Sunset Cove

ANJ Press

Pittsburgh

SUNSET COVE

ANJ Press, First edition. December 2021.

Copyright © 2021 Amelia Addler.

Written by Amelia Addler.

Cover design by CrocoDesigns

Maps by MistyBeee

For the hope of new beginnings

Introduction to *Sunset Cove*

A six-million-dollar inheritance, and a chance at a new life...

At 52, Claire Cooke gets the shock of a lifetime when she's named the sole heir of a distant uncle. As a single mom, she's already had to watch her kids grow up and leave the nest, so Claire decides to keep the money and take a risk: she buys The Grand Madrona Hotel on beautiful Orcas Island and prepares for a new chapter in her life.

Chip Douglas didn't put in ten years as manager of the hotel just to watch a stranger run it into the ground. So imagine his surprise when Claire turns out to be the exact opposite of what he'd expected. She's charming, wise, and beautiful – someone he could easily see himself falling in love with. If only his divorce hadn't convinced him that falling in love again was impossible...

When the FBI shows up at Claire's door asking questions about a dangerous criminal with close ties to her past, it's not long before Claire is forced to face her history or lose her potentially happily ever after with Chip. Will she make the right choice?

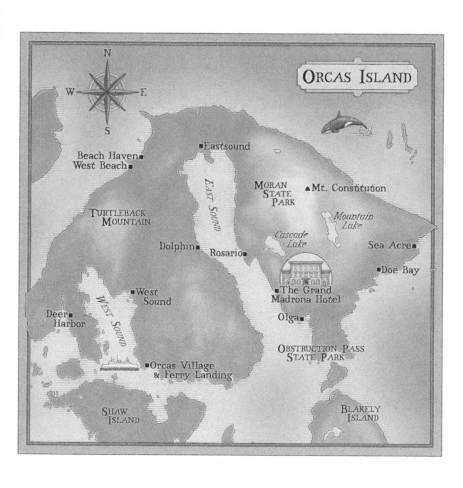

Chapter One

A blast rang out and Claire popped up from her pillow. It was dark in the unfamiliar hotel room as she strained to listen through the hollow silence.

Voices carried through the door and a moment later, she heard the clamoring of dishes. Her heart was still racing as the room service cart clanked by.

Claire let out a sigh. The sound had been real, not imagined. She hadn't startled herself awake from a dream this time, the same one she'd dreamt a thousand times.

It had variations, of course. Sometimes she was onboard the small single-engine plane, screaming as she felt a force pulling her down, down, down, before exploding in a flash of light.

Other times, she dreamt she was on the ground, watching as the little aircraft's wings clipped the tops of the trees before slamming into the side of a mountain.

No matter how it started, the outcome was always the same – fire, confusion, and a lack of survivors. Just like it had been in real life.

New chapters in life often started with a crash. Claire knew that. She was trying to avoid any crashes, collapses, or otherwise destructive starts this time, however. She hoped that her new beginning on Orcas Island would go smoothly. Quietly. That she'd be in control.

As much as that was possible. She rolled over to check the time on her phone, but despite pushing its buttons and giving it a shake, it refused to wake up. She squinted in the darkness and saw that the phone charger was hanging loosely from the outlet.

Ah. Loose outlets weren't uncommon in old buildings like this. It was just another improvement they needed to make. She marked it down in her notebook.

The list was growing quite long, as she'd expected. It'd been nearly a week since she'd closed on the sale of The Grand Madrona Hotel, and she'd spent each night in a different room, taking notes, admiring the views, and finding out that many of the hotel's critical reviews held nuggets of truth.

Her neck and shoulders were stiff from an anxious night, and she stretched before hopping out of bed and scooting across the creaking hardwood floor. She liked the sound; there was a charm to the hotel, something that she didn't want to lose. The 1920's style sang through the little details: the eloquent tile patterns, the gold-trimmed banisters. It just needed a bit of polish to really shine.

She pulled the curtains open with a dramatic swoop and the sunlight peeked in. This was the best room in the hotel – the Sunset Suite. The placid ocean waters filled her view and, in the distance, tiny green trees rose to the sky, a thousand perfect brushstrokes on the mountainside.

With some effort, Claire managed to open the old window and take a breath of the crisp island air. The sunlight quieted the jittery thoughts in her head, and she felt the fear of the morning fizzling away.

Claire smiled to herself. So what if she didn't know anything about running a hotel? These views sold themselves! How hard could it be?

Not that hard – at least not yet, though she was open to suggestions. Claire had hired a hospitality consultant who told her to spend at least one night in every room of the hotel. He argued that she needed a true idea of what the experience was like for guests, and since there were only thirty-two rooms, it didn't seem too cumbersome.

This was her sixth night, and she was glad she'd saved the suite until now. The room was more spacious than the others, and the furnishings were more grand. Best of all was the gentle sound of the water lapping at the shore – she'd never grow sick of it.

The night before, she'd sat in front of the window and watched as the sun set behind Turtleback Mountain, turning the sky from a smattering of orange and red, to yellow, and finally a glowing blue.

It was a perfect place, better than a dream. Claire leaned out of the window and closed her eyes.

There was a knock at the door. "Housekeeping!"

Did housekeeping always come this early? She leaned forward to grab her watch from the desk and startled at the time. It was nearly nine o'clock!

She'd promised to be out by eight so that housekeeping could get the room ready for the next paying customer.

"Just a few minutes, please!" Claire called out. She was supposed to meet the general manager, Charles – or did he go by Chip? – at nine for their first formal appointment. He'd been out the week prior visiting family for the holidays, and she was excited to finally talk to him.

Claire needed to make a good impression on Chip. The previous owner, Steve, said that the hotel lived and died by the manager's orders.

She got dressed and hastily threw her bag together, slinging it over her shoulder before catching the elevator down to the lobby.

This was perhaps her favorite spot in the hotel. Everything about it just felt right – the sleek marble floors, the art deco furniture, the chandelier that hung over the elegant, sweeping staircase.

Most miraculously of all, this stunning place was *hers*.

Gigi was manning the front desk – sort of. Her head was bowed down, eyes fixed on her cell phone, and all Claire could see was her black hair.

Claire walked up to the desk, apparently unnoticed, and cleared her throat. Gigi looked up from her phone before letting out a sigh. "Good morning."

"Good morning!" Claire said as she heaved her bag onto the table. "Would you be able to store this for me? I'm not sure if my next room is ready yet."

Gigi looked at the computer screen, clicking away. "Doesn't look like it. I can let you know when it is."

"Thanks Gigi. Oh! Have you seen Charles around?"

Gigi frowned. "Do you mean Chip?"

"Er – yes. I wasn't sure everyone called him that, or if it was just a nickname that Steve had made up."

"No one ever calls him Charles," she said flatly. "That won't win you any points."

Claire smiled. "Got it. Have you seen Chip, then?"

"I don't think so," she said with a shrug.

Claire could tell that Gigi was quickly losing interest in this conversation – if she ever had any interest in it to begin with. "I'll see if I can find him. Will you please call me when my new room is ready?"

"It's going to be a while. Housekeeping fell behind this morning."

News traveled fast, didn't it? "Ah, sure. No problem. I'll wait for your call."

Gigi nodded, her head already drifting, eyes fixed downward.

Claire rushed into the hotel's restaurant, The Plum Spoon, but Chip was nowhere to be seen. She was only a few minutes late. Surely he hadn't already marked her as a lost cause?

Claire was seated and she plugged her phone charger into a nearby wall. This time, the charger managed to hold.

She then turned her attention to trying to tame her disheveled hair using her reflection in the window. It was in vain – her hair had stubbornly decided its place for the day – and before long, the waiter stopped by to get her order.

She'd had the same waiter every day so far – Dan. He was a pleasant younger guy who gushed with excitement about both things to do on Orcas Island, as well as whatever the restaurant was serving that day. That morning, he was talking up the special: an oyster omelette.

Seafood didn't sound appetizing to her anxious stomach. Yet Dan told her that the oysters were caught locally, that they had a sweeter taste than most, and how the chef expertly prepared only the best ones. She finally relented and said she'd love to try it.

Her omelette arrived quickly, garnished with a beautiful flower and flanked by fresh fruit on one side and lightly fried potatoes on the other. Claire found the fruit and potatoes easiest to stomach, but she took small bites of the omelette as well.

No need to offend Dan or the restaurant owner – they were just about the only people who had been nice to her in the past week, and if they decided to stop renting the space, Claire would have a hard time finding a restaurant to fill the void.

She kept checking her phone to see if she had any messages from Chip. Perhaps she'd gotten the day wrong, or something awful had happened to him? A car accident? A ferry accident?

She was about to call his cell phone when he walked through the door of the restaurant, a frown fixed on his face.

Claire stood up and waved. "Hey there!"

He saw her and nodded. "Miss Cooke, it's good to see you."

"Please," she said, waving a hand. "Call me Claire."

He looked different than she remembered, though she'd only met him for a brief moment before when she was talking to the previous owner.

He was dressed differently then, in a thickly knit sweater, and Steve had teased that he'd have to trade it in for a suit and tie once Claire was in charge.

Chip hadn't gone as far as all that, but he was wearing a button-down shirt which seemed to fit awkwardly around his biceps, the material taut and strained.

Maybe that was why he looked so grouchy? His clothes were too tight. He was a big guy, at least a head taller than Claire, and far too broad to be struggling against a flimsy shirt all day.

That must be it – tight clothes. That could set anyone on edge.

They shook hands, his large hand squeezing hers firmly, and he took a seat. "I'm sorry for being late – "

Claire rushed to respond. "That's no problem, I had a bit of a late start myself today. I hope nothing is wrong?"

"No." His scowl deepened. "Just a guest threatening to leave a one-star review."

"Oh no! What happened?"

He shook his head, and Dan stopped by to take his order. "Just coffee, thanks." Chip sat back. "Nothing to worry about. He was caught smoking in his room – lit part of the duvet on fire. We had to charge him the two-hundred-dollar cleaning fee, and I had half a mind to drag the duvet into the lobby for him to add to his review."

Claire winced.

"What?" Chip said. "Would you have preferred if I handled it a different way?"

"No, I wouldn't say that, I just – "

"What?" He crossed his arms.

Claire bit her lip. "It's nothing. I don't have any experience in hospitality, as you know."

"Yes, I know."

She forced a smile. "I'm not sure if Steve told you, but I ended up hiring a consultant – Ken Gallon? Have you worked with him before, or maybe read his book?"

Chip shook his head. "Never heard of him."

"Oh, well, he recommended that I read a few books about hospitality. They talk about different ways to handle challenging situations."

"Do they?" he said, accepting his coffee with a nod.

Claire paused. This wasn't how she'd hoped this meeting would go. "Maybe we can set up a time to talk about that later? I'm sure that you've had a lot of experience in dealing with difficult customers."

"Yes, I have." Chip took a sip of his coffee before setting it down in front of him. "But if that's how you think I would best spend my time, then I guess that's what I'll be doing."

All right then. Clearly Claire was not doing well in keeping the hotel's right-hand man happy. "No – please. I want *you* to tell me what we need to do. I was hoping to learn a lot from you."

"Look," he said, leaning forward. "I'm going to level with you. Things at the hotel don't look good."

She sat back. "What do you mean?"

"It's not been a great time for hotels the last few years, if you haven't noticed."

Claire nodded. "Oh, of course."

"I'm not trying to say that Steve painted an overly rosy picture of our financial situation here. He genuinely believed in the place. To be honest, he probably thought it would all work out, like it always had. I couldn't get him to listen to me."

"I'll listen to you," Claire said quickly. "Really."

He reached into his bag and pulled out a file. "Take a look for yourself. I've prepared some reports. There's a list of expenses, a few pages on the budget, and the projected occupancy for the coming year. At the end there's a list of suggested improvements –"

"Oh yes, I've got some ideas for improvements, too," she said, pulling her notebook out of her purse.

He narrowed his eyes at the notebook, reading off her first suggestion. "New curtains? It's going to take more than that to keep this place going."

Claire nodded, covering her silly notebook with the papers he'd just given her. She flipped to the end of the packet, eager to see the improvements he'd listed.

Eager wasn't the most honest word – she was also afraid. She'd spent most of her money buying the hotel, and though she'd set aside some money for improvements, the idea frightened her. Spending money was always hard for her, especially because for most of her life, she'd hardly had any.

"You look overwhelmed," said Chip. "Do you want me to talk you through some of this?"

"That would be great," said Claire, looking up with a smile.

Dan appeared at the end of the table. "Excuse me, Miss Cooke?"

"Dan, please, it's Claire."

He flashed a smile.

"What's up?" she asked.

"I'm sorry to interrupt, but I think someone is looking for you."

"Oh?"

He dropped his voice. "They said they were FBI agents."

Claire laughed, but his expression didn't change. "I'm sorry. Are you serious?"

He nodded his head. "They asked for you at the front desk, but now they're running around the hotel. I think some of the guests are upset."

Claire stood up. "Wow, okay." She looked down at Chip. "Some of the staff has been pulling jokes on me. All in good fun, you know, but at first I assumed..." She flashed a smile and let out a sigh. "I'm sorry, Chip. I'd better go and see what this is about. Maybe we can –"

Chip nodded. "I'll be in my office when you're done."

Claire offered him a strained smile. "Thanks."

Chapter Two

C hip stared at Claire's back as she walked away.

Unbelievable.

Their first meeting had lasted all of fifteen minutes. When Steve sold the hotel, he assured Chip that he was leaving the place in good hands.

It didn't seem that way. It seemed like Steve had gotten soft in his old age.

"No, he was always soft," Chip muttered to himself. The old man had hired him ten years ago, even though he had no experience in hotels. Steve had taught him everything he knew – well, sort of. Chip always knew more about money than Steve did. Steve never cared about money, hence the state the hotel was in now.

Chip let out a sigh. Claire had left behind the papers he'd given her, and she didn't pay for her breakfast. He debated adding her meal to his tab, but decided that would seem too much like he was kissing up.

He'd tried to be considerate of her when he decided to wear a "nice" shirt. Chip had regretted that from the moment he left the house. It was uncomfortable, and it felt weird. Why should he have to change how he dressed because of a new owner? Steve never cared how he dressed.

He paid for his coffee and walked out to the lobby, spotting a distracted Gigi at the front desk.

"Gigi. Off your phone," he snapped. "I'm going to start locking it up if you can't keep your eyes off of it."

"Sorry boss," she said with a smile. "Hey, did you hear?"

"Hear what?"

Her eyes brightened and she leaned forward. "That the new owner is a criminal."

Chip frowned. "What?"

Linda, the events coordinator, popped up behind him. "I bet that's how she got the money to buy the hotel. Do you think she's in with the mob or something?"

"No, I don't think she's in with the mob," Chip said.

Gigi nodded. "Yeah, you're probably right. She's too clueless. I think she's just a rich lady who's never worked a day in her life."

Linda nodded. "I can see that."

Gigi dropped her voice. "Did you know that she's spending a night in every room? It's driving housekeeping nuts. Every time I think they have a freebie because the room was empty, Claire messes it up."

"Can't wait for my meeting with her," Linda said airily.

Chip said nothing and walked off. He had his questions, too, but he wasn't going to join in the staff gossip. It didn't matter who this woman was – they had to deal with her regardless.

She was the new owner of the hotel, the hotel that he had dedicated the last ten years of his life to, the same one that had been in a spiral for the last two years. A spiral that Claire seemed bent on accelerating.

When he handed her the numbers – the facts of her new situation – she looked at him like he'd dumped a glass of water over her head.

Chip smiled to himself. He'd sort of wanted that reaction. He wanted her to feel shocked, surprised, and overwhelmed. Sometimes people need to get a little jolt to move them into action.

He needed her to understand how serious the situation was at the hotel, how close they all were to being bought up by a huge company and their roles "streamlined" in the name of profit.

Fifteen minutes wasn't enough to communicate this to her, though, especially when she had her own list of ideas for improvement. As if a week at the hotel was all she needed to figure it out!

Ridiculous. How could she think that she knew better than him? Because she'd hired a consultant?

Chip got back to his office and looked up the consultant, this Mr. Ken Gallon. The guy was clearly a grifter. His résumé read like a list of schemes, jumping from one strangely named company to the next. He used overly flowery language, saying that while employed at a bank he "managed portfolios totaling over fifty million dollars."

What did that even mean? That the bank had fifty million? That was nothing for a bank. When Chip had worked at an investment bank, he saw hundreds of millions of dollars disappear like it was nothing.

And now the FBI was poking around his hotel. Despite not knowing for certain that it was Claire's fault that federal agents were there, he was angry enough to assign her the full blame. He huffed around his office, shuttling papers, moving books, and muttering to himself.

In his fury, he knocked an old mug of coffee onto his copy of the financials.

"Well, that's just great," he said, mopping up the mess with a paper towel.

So much for his plan for the next year. He tossed the sopping paper towel into the trash and took a seat. "It'll be a miracle if we even make it a year," he muttered, turning to his computer.

Chapter Three

After checking the gym, the banquet hall, and the lengths of the first and second floors, Claire was beginning to wonder if perhaps she'd dismissed the prank theory too quickly.

There was no sign of the alleged FBI agents anywhere, and the look on Chip's face as she walked away was burned into her mind's eye – the look of disappointment. Or was it disgust?

Claire wasn't sure, but it was bad. Steve made it sound like Chip was the most important person at the hotel. How was she going to make any of this work without his help?

The elevator let out a ding – a light, metallic sound that Claire couldn't get enough of – and the doors opened to the third floor. She looked around, seeing no one. The housekeeping cart was parked outside of the Sunset Suite, and Claire decided she'd ask them if they'd seen anyone. If they hadn't, she'd give up her futile search.

She walked through the doorway and stopped in her tracks. One man was pulling out the desk drawers, and a second was on his knees, looking under the bed.

"Is everything okay in here?" Claire asked in her small, trying-to-be-the-boss voice.

The man halfway under the bed popped up and flashed a smile. "Hi there. I'm Special Agent Alvarez, and this is Special Agent McCoy. We're with the FBI."

So much for it being a prank. "Hi! Nice to meet you. I'm Claire. Claire Cooke."

Agent Alvarez shook her hand, as did Agent McCoy. Claire stared at them, a smile frozen on her face.

"Just the lady we were hoping to meet," Agent Alvarez said. "Is there somewhere we can go to talk?"

"Yes, of course. Is something wrong? We can talk here, no problem, anywhere you like." She lowered herself onto a nearby chair.

Rhonda, the housekeeper, popped out of the bathroom. "Gigi said that the guests for this room requested an early check-in."

"Oh," Claire nodded, shooting up from her seat. "Of course. Sorry Rhonda. Ah – let's talk downstairs."

They both smiled and followed her out of the room. Claire led them down the hallway and into the elevator, her mind racing.

Had a guest gone missing or something? Did she file her taxes wrong? That wouldn't be the FBI, though.

Unless...perhaps her jump from a salary of less than sixty thousand dollars a year to a windfall of six million dollars was exactly the sort of thing the FBI looked into?

Once the elevator doors shut, she couldn't help herself. "Is everything okay? Did something happen to my girls?"

"Oh no, nothing like that. Don't worry yourself," said Agent Alvarez. "But we do have some concerns about your son."

Ding! The doors opened into the lobby.

"My son?" Claire said slowly, taking a step out. "I don't have a son."

The agents shot each other a look before motioning forward; there were people waiting to get in the elevator. Claire apologized and got out of the way.

The only office in the hotel was Chip's office. Theoretically, there was a desk for her in there, too, but Chip wouldn't thank her for kicking him out. Instead she led the agents to the banquet hall which was, thankfully, empty.

"Please, have a seat," she said, motioning to a table on the far side of the room. The floor-to-ceiling windows revealed a stunning view of the water. It dazzled Claire every time she walked into this room, though this time she was too distracted to appreciate it fully.

"Thank you," said Agent McCoy. "Miss Cooke, like Agent Alvarez mentioned, we're here to talk to you about your son."

She shifted in her seat. "Yes, but as I've said, I don't have a son. I have three daughters – Lucy, Lillian, and Rose."

Agent Alvarez pulled a sheet of paper from his briefcase and slid it across the table. "Do you recognize this, Miss Cooke?"

She leaned forward. It looked like it was from the ancestry company where she'd sent her DNA test. The girls had gotten it for her for Christmas – they thought it would be fun to see if they had any long-lost ancestors.

"It looks like the test I got for Christmas, but I haven't gotten the results yet." She frowned. There was a lot of information on there.

"Yes, these are the results of your DNA test. You submitted your saliva for this test, right?"

She nodded. "Yes, I did."

"Well," he continued, "we got a match in our database to your results. To your son, who we need to talk to."

"I don't have a son," she insisted. "I've never had any children."

Agent McCoy raised an eyebrow. "You just said you have three daughters. Or do they not exist anymore?"

Claire let out a sigh. "They're my adopted daughters. I mean I don't have any *biological* children. I've never had a son, adopted or otherwise."

It was a point that one of the moms in Lucy's kindergarten liked to harp on back in the day. "You'll never understand," she once told Claire, "until you have a *real* child, one of your own."

Claire's stomach churned at the memory. The girls *were* her real children, and she was a real mom. Comments like that had haunted her for years, though, and made her question herself more than she wanted to admit.

"Okay." Agent McCoy sat back, nodding. "So you adopted three girls, but no boys?"

She didn't like the tone of his voice, but he was clearly wrong and would feel silly when he realized his mistake. "Yes. Three girls, my sister's daughters. She died in a plane crash twenty-nine years ago this March. It was in Colorado. I'm sure you can find it, in the papers maybe, or –"

"We'll get right on that," Agent McCoy said with a smile. "What I want to focus on right now is that your son is in trouble. But you know that, don't you? Has he tried to contact you?"

Her eyes darted between them. "I'm sorry, but you have the wrong person. The company must have made a mistake with the results."

"The company assured us that they don't make mistakes."

She let out a sigh. "I'm pretty sure I would remember being pregnant and having a son."

Agent Alvarez smiled before he spoke, his voice soft. "When did he come to see you? Is he staying here?"

It was like talking to a wall! Maybe this *was* a prank, an especially cruel one. Why hadn't she asked to see their badges?

"I don't know who you're talking about," Claire said.

Agent McCoy shook his head. "We know that he was last seen nearby, in Anacortes. We think that he wanted to meet you."

"Meet *me?*"

"He knows that you're his birth mother," Agent Alvarez added. "We assumed he came to meet you."

She raised her eyebrows. Birth mother? This was perhaps the cruelest trick anyone had ever pulled on her. She couldn't even form a response.

Agent McCoy let out a dramatic sigh and stood up. "DNA doesn't lie, Claire. Here's my card. How about you get in touch with us when you're ready to talk?"

She reached forward and picked up the card from the table. It looked official, not that she'd be able to tell at this point. Her mind was in a tailspin as the agents walked away.

"But if you wait too long," he added, looking over his shoulder, "we won't be able to help you."

By the time she looked up again, they were gone. She stared at the card in her hand. It had his name, an office phone, and a cell phone. That seemed like a lot for a prank.

What did he mean that DNA didn't lie? She didn't care what the company said. They'd made a mistake!

Claire stood up, pacing the room. What was she supposed to do? What if some criminal actually *did* come looking for her? She could call the FBI guy, but it might be too late.

What kind of crime were they investigating? Maybe if the guy thought she was his mother, he wouldn't hurt her. Unless he was bitter that she'd abandoned him.

Claire sat down at the table again, the room spinning around her.

Chapter Four

It had been half an hour. Claire was blowing him off, and Chip didn't have all day to wait around for a meeting with her. Steve never used to keep him waiting – he was always available when someone needed him.

Chip got up from his desk, taking both packets with him. She wasn't in the lobby or the restaurant. No sign of her out on the patio, either. He was about to get on the elevator when Linda caught his arm.

"If you're looking for Claire, she's in the banquet hall."

"I was. Thanks."

Linda tightened her grip. "I tried to eavesdrop. It was hard to hear, but those FBI agents were *not* happy with her."

"They can get in line," Chip said firmly before walking off.

Claire was inside, as promised, staring at her phone. This was why she'd kept him waiting? So she could play Gigi in the corner?

"You forgot your papers," he said.

She jumped a little, then looked up at him. "Oh my gosh, I'm so sorry. Thank you."

"Are you ready to go over them, or...?"

"Actually, now's not really a good time," Claire said, standing up. "I need to, ah, take care of some things. I'm really sorry."

"If it's more important than the survival of the hotel, sure."

She looked down, then back up at him. "It's not more important than that, I just – can we set up a time tomorrow to talk?"

The nerve of this lady! Like he didn't have better things to do than chase her around and plead with her to take her new business seriously.

"I guess we can do tomorrow." He crossed his arms. "Unless you expect the FBI to haul you away."

Claire nodded, brushing past him. "Anytime. Please let me know."

He was about to snap something back at her when her phone rang. She answered it.

"Hello?"

Chip gritted his teeth. She was ignoring him *again!*

"Slow down, sweetie. What happened?" Claire listened, her forehead crinkling. "Lucy, honey, please don't cry. It's not worth it to –"

He stared at her, cradling the phone to her ear with her shoulder as she clutched the pile of reports to her chest. Was she talking to her daughter?

For the first time, Chip had the strange, creeping thought that she wasn't just the new hotel owner – she was also a regular human being.

"Okay," Claire said softly, "No, that's fine. Call me any time. I love you."

As she tried to move the phone into her pocket, she dropped all of the papers onto the ballroom's dance floor. They spun around her, floating to the floor in a ragged pile.

"Oh gosh, sorry," she muttered, dropping to the ground.

It was as though someone had tossed a bucket of water onto the raging flame in Chip's mind. He'd allowed himself to get entirely too worked up at this poor woman.

On the ground, Claire was frantic, dropping half of the papers again, almost falling as she tried to gather them. He knelt down to help her, but before he could think of something to say, she thanked him, apologized again, and disappeared from his sight.

Chapter Five

T hings weren't adding up. As much as Claire didn't want to further annoy Chip, she had to get away from the hotel and find a quiet place. She needed to call the DNA company, or the FBI, or anyone who could get to the bottom of this misunderstanding.

Claire was already in her car and halfway down the road from the hotel when she realized that she'd forgotten her overnight bag. She slammed on the brakes.

Wait. Did she even need the bag? She closed her eyes and told herself to stop being flustered. It was hard for her. Occasionally when someone yelled at her, especially with so much anger, it threw her back into being a young, clueless paralegal.

At her first job, Claire would get screamed at for everything – using the wrong font on a document, scheduling meetings for too long of a time, scheduling meetings for too short of a time...

The job was a nightmare, but Claire had needed it, and she had needed the paycheck to keep her and the girls from being evicted. The abuse worked just as intended, too. For far too long, she was convinced that she couldn't hack it at another job, so she stayed and suffered.

It sounded like her daughter Lucy was having a similar experience. She'd just called from the bathroom at her job, near tears, telling Claire that she'd been yelled at in front of the entire staff.

Poor Lucy. Claire's stomach tightened. It didn't matter how old her kids were, she still wanted to rescue them, swooping in with a Band-Aid and a kiss. If only it were that easy.

More and more these days, she was finding it impossible to help her kids. Their problems were too big and, further, they didn't ask for her help.

Even Lucy hadn't really needed her just then. Claire had hardly said a word. Lucy made up her mind to go back and fight for herself on her own.

It made Claire feel...lost. She was proud of her girls, of course, but it felt like her purpose was slipping away.

She opened her eyes and let out a deep breath. No one was chasing her now. Everything was fine. She didn't need that bag unless she was planning to flee the island and never come back.

Claire smiled. That would be silly. And it would look suspicious to the FBI.

Not that she needed to worry about looking suspicious to the FBI. She'd done nothing wrong. More concerning was the criminal who was convinced she was his mother.

One problem at a time, though. Claire took her foot off the brake and continued her drive.

It was quite a journey to her rental cabin. Perhaps it wasn't the best place to stay, but Claire hadn't realized just how long it took to get from one side of the horseshoe-shaped island to the other – in her case, over half an hour, door-to-door.

It was her own fault. In all of her excitement over buying the hotel, Claire hadn't put much thought into where she'd be living. Her friend Margie, who lived on nearby San Juan Island, had helped her secure a place just a few weeks prior.

There weren't many rentals on the island, but Margie knew someone – Margie *always* knew someone – who was happy to rent her the little cabin at an extremely reasonable price.

"Any friend of Margie's is a friend of mine," the guy had said. "Besides, we hardly ever use the cabin anymore. We built a little house on Lopez Island, a place without stairs or ladders. Easier on the knees."

Claire loved the cabin. It was rustic, but cozy. She didn't mind the ladder that led up to the loft; she didn't mind that the heat didn't quite work. It felt private. Serene.

The drive gave her more time to calm down and sort her thoughts. She'd never been in any trouble before, and surely if the FBI was looking into her now, they'd see that she'd never had a kid. If not, how could she prove that something hadn't happened?

Claire stopped at the base of the private road to collect her mail. There was an impressive pile, though most of it looked like junk.

Before continuing, she peered over her shoulder. No one had followed her. That was good.

The driveway was a quarter mile to the cabin, and the road was so long and winding that she was sure she was alone. As she rolled along, the gravel pinging her car, her mind calmed even more.

The little cabin sat on sixteen acres of land, all trees and dense brush and ancient-looking ferns. When she got inside, she did a cursory check of the spaces – the loft, the open kitchen and living room, the bedroom and bathroom. It was so small that there was nowhere for a criminal would-be son to hide.

Good. Claire put on some water for tea and pulled out her phone, plugging it in to charge before making a call to the company who had mishandled her DNA. After a frustrating seven minutes of pressing buttons and speaking to a robot, she finally reached a person.

Unfortunately, the person wasn't much more helpful than the robot. The company representative kept repeating that she couldn't disclose any information related to an ongoing investigation.

"Even if it's *my* alleged DNA that's been implicated in the investigation?" asked Claire.

"I'm sorry, ma'am, but I'm not at liberty to say one way or the other. By sending us your sample, you consented to having your genetic makeup put into a database and made available to law enforcement."

Claire let out a sigh. "But there's been some sort of mistake. I'd like you to take my name out of this database – and my DNA."

There was silence for a moment. "I'm not sure that that's possible, but I can have someone call you."

Claire went around and around with the representative for almost ten minutes before finally saying, "That's all for today, thank you."

How had the FBI gotten the results before she did? Apparently, when Claire had sent off that vial of saliva, she sent every last scrap of her privacy with it.

Claire set down her tea and went over to inspect the pile of mail, hoping to find her results. Most of it was junk – advertisements, a flyer for pizza, and coupons. Nothing from the DNA company.

There was one letter that stuck out. It had her address hand-written onto it. There was no return address, and no name.

How odd. She tore the envelope open and pulled out the paper inside. As she unfolded it, something fell out and onto the floor.

Claire frowned and knelt down to pick it up. It was a Polaroid picture, face side down. She turned it in her hand and gasped.

It was a picture of her holding a baby, seemingly from many years ago. She flipped it over and back again, looking for a date or description, but there was nothing. She stared at the face in the picture for a moment before realizing that it wasn't her, but her twin sister Rebecca.

Claire sat down on the couch, almost missing the cushion, as her heart rate picked up.

No, there was no mistaking it. It was absolutely her twin sister. Whose baby was that? Becca had never had a baby, and she'd died in the plane crash, too. She was the reason that her family was in that plane in the first place, to pick her up from a rehab facility in the mountains.

Prior to the rehab visit, Becca had been missing for over a year. She'd gone completely off the grid, and more than once they'd worried that she was dead.

Claire shook her head. She remembered that frantic phone call from Becca, saying that she was going to run off and none of them would ever see her again unless they took her out of that place immediately.

"Tell Mom and Dad they've got twenty-four hours, or I'm gone forever."

Becca was always putting pressure on their parents like that. It had annoyed Claire to no end. She was home on spring break from law school, and after relaying the threat, she freely told her parents her opinion on the matter. "You should stop giving in to her. If she wants to run away, let her run away."

"We can't lose her, Claire," her mom said sternly before making a call to Claire's older sister Holly. Her husband Rob was a pilot at an airline, and he had a friend with a small single-engine plane. He had offered to fly them all down there to talk Becca out of her tantrum...

And so it went. The weather was bad, the plane had mechanical issues, and they crashed. The girls had lost their parents and their grandparents in one moment, all in the name of saving Becca a final time.

Yet seeing this picture brought up an old, dusty paranoia from Claire's mind. It was a nagging feeling, an intrusive thought that never gave her rest. It poked and prodded, over and over: what if Becca had survived?

Her body was never found, though neither was Claire's mother's. The terrain was so treacherous that rescuers had to stop searching for their own safety. It, along with a strange feeling in her chest, left just enough of a seed of doubt in Claire's mind, though.

When was this picture taken? She flipped it over again, desperate to find a date, but there was nothing. Becca looked different. Healthier. Happy, even. She was holding the baby in her arms and half smiling in her cool way.

Still dumbfounded, Claire reached for the letter.

"Do you remember me? I would like to meet again. I will be at Mountain Lake on January 2nd at dusk. The dock near the parking lot. I hope to see you there."

She read the letter three times before realizing that the date had already passed. She'd completely missed it!

Why hadn't she had her mail forwarded to the hotel? Probably because Gigi would've thrown it right in the trash.

Her stomach dropped. Apparently, whoever this guy was, he knew where she lived. How could he know where she lived? Claire barely knew it herself!

There was a noise outside, and she nearly jumped off of the couch.

Even the most level-headed person can feel like the earth is splitting beneath their feet with the right mix of fear and bizarre occurrences. Claire could only take so much.

She grabbed her purse and bolted, running from the cracks in her world that threatened to swallow her whole.

Chapter Six

T he January air was brisk, and it was another magnificent day on Westcott Bay. Margie stepped outside, her thick coat wrapped tightly around her, a hot mug of coffee in her hands. It was her second cup of the day – she knew that she shouldn't, but she was out of hot chocolate and needed something with heft.

She'd finally finished cleaning the house after having all of the kids over for Christmas. It was a grand, marvelous affair. Margie's eggnog was a hit, as were all of the new recipes she'd debuted – the sesame shrimp pastry puffs, the crab fettuccine, and even the squash and caramelized onion tart.

Everyone seemed to enjoy themselves, so much so that no fights broke out – not even a single argument! Margie was glad for that, of course. In a way it made her sad, because it showed how much all of the kids had grown up.

With her two daughters married off, though, she was hopeful there would soon be a new generation of troublemakers coming her way.

"Psst!"

There was a rustling in the trees to the side of the house. Margie narrowed her eyes. It felt like she was being accosted by an odd bird.

"Over here!" said a ragged voice.

Margie walked over, carefully stepping over rocks before finding her friend Claire hiding behind a tree. "Claire! What are you doing back there?"

Claire's eyes darted left, then right, then back over her shoulder. "I don't want to put you in danger."

"In danger?" Margie repeated before letting out a booming laugh.

Claire shushed her again. "I'm serious! The FBI was looking for me. There might be someone else, too." She fidgeted with her hands. "Do you have cameras on your property?"

"Do I have cameras...? No! Of course not."

Claire clenched her hands in front of her chest. "I shouldn't have come here. I'm sorry, Margie."

"Now hang on," Margie said, reaching forward to pick a leaf out of Claire's hair.

Margie knew someone who'd had a nervous breakdown once – a distant relative who wasn't pleasant even on a good day. It was hard to say for sure, but it seemed like Claire was exhibiting symptoms of something similar.

This just wasn't Claire's normal, sweet self. Claire was one of the most level-headed people that Margie knew! When the girls were growing up, Margie would get herself into a tizzy over just about anything, while Claire, with her quiet composure, could always keep her cool.

Something had to be very wrong.

"Why don't we go inside," Margie said gently, "and talk this out?"

Claire shook her head. "I can't. It might be dangerous."

Margie let out a tut before unzipping her jacket and putting it over Claire's shoulders. "Don't be ridiculous. I'm married to the chief deputy sheriff, my brother was in the FBI, and it can't be worse than the time I had a card-carrying member of the mob break into my house."

Claire raised an eyebrow. "A member of the mob broke into your house?"

"We had a taser," Margie said, waving a hand. She was long past that sort of excitement in her own life. "It was fine. There's nothing to be afraid of. Let's go inside."

Claire offered her a pained smile before giving into Margie's grip and walking toward the house.

Once they were inside, Margie made up a mug of coffee with a dollop of cream and sugar for Claire before forcing it into her hands.

"Now *talk*," Margie said.

Claire let out a sigh before telling her about a strange, albeit unthreatening, visit from two FBI agents that morning.

"Clearly they just made a mistake," Margie said soothingly. Her brother Mike had been in the FBI. Surely he still had some connections. "I'm sure Mike can sort it out."

"Can you even reach him?" Claire asked.

Margie tapped her chin. He'd set off to sail the world, but he checked in every few weeks. Usually.

"Of course I can," said Margie, voice too high.

Claire let out a sigh. "It gets worse. Look at this."

Margie accepted an envelope from her before carefully opening it and peering inside. There was an old Polaroid picture of Claire.

"Aw, look how cute you were!" Margie squealed.

Claire shook her head. "That's not me, Margie. That's Rebecca."

Margie frowned. "Oh. Right. I'm sorry."

"Look at the letter that came with it."

Margie smiled as she unfolded it, reading it once, then again, her smile fading. "Claire! What is this?"

"I think it's a letter from Rebecca's son."

"You never told me Rebecca had a son."

"Rebecca never told *me* that she had a son."

Margie stared at her friend, mouth open. So much for not working herself into a tizzy. She was well on her way. "What does this mean, Claire?"

"I don't know." Claire took a sip of her coffee. "I don't know how she could've hidden this from us. I have no idea when this picture was taken."

Margie stared at the picture again. Perhaps now she could convince herself that this wasn't a picture of her friend, though she surely wouldn't have known the difference if Claire hadn't told her. They had been identical, after all, despite their personalities being polar opposites.

"Well," Margie said. "That's quite a secret she kept."

Claire nodded. "I'm not surprised. I mean, of course I'm shocked, but I'm not *surprised*. Becca lived so erratically, so... I don't know. So differently than I have. It's strange, but I've always wondered if..."

Claire trailed off, staring into the mug.

Margie inched closer. "What?"

"This is going to sound silly," Claire said with a sigh. "I've always wondered if Becca survived the plane crash."

Margie sat back, trying to hide the surprise on her face. "Why?"

Claire shrugged. "It's just a feeling that I've had. You know how they never found her body?"

Margie nodded.

"I could see her just running away from it all," Claire said. "What if she had this boy after the crash? Just gave him away and disappeared?"

"I'm guessing you didn't go to the park to meet him last week, then?" asked Margie.

"No, I didn't open this letter until today. I panicked, thinking that he might be lurking in the woods and that he's some sort of serial killer."

Margie laughed. "So you came here."

"Yes." Claire nodded. "I came here. I'm so sorry, I shouldn't have –"

"Nonsense," Margie said, smiling warmly. "I've said it before, and I'll say it again. I'm not afraid."

Claire offered a sad smile.

Margie continued. "I don't think that this boy is coming to kill you. If he'd wanted to kill you, he probably would've done it already."

Claire, wide-eyed, turned to her. "Margie!"

She put her hands up. "Oh, you know what I mean! It looks like he just wants to meet you."

"Maybe." Claire bit her lip.

"Did the FBI say why they were looking for him?"

Claire shook her head. "No, and I didn't think to ask. They were so angry with me. They were convinced I was lying."

"Hm." Margie rapped her fingers on her now empty mug. "They didn't say that he was armed and dangerous. Maybe they want him for...tax evasion."

"Tax evasion?" Claire raised an eyebrow.

Margie brightened. "Like Al Capone."

Claire cracked a smile. "Al Capone, the famous, violent mobster? Do you think Becca's son is a mobster?"

"Gosh, I hope not!" Margie stood up. "I don't want you to worry about this. I can have Hank check at the station and –"

"No," Claire put a hand up. "I know this is a lot to ask, but please don't tell him about this. Not yet. Not until I figure it out."

Margie frowned. It was hard, if not impossible, to keep secrets from her husband Hank. Margie wasn't great at keeping secrets in general.

At the same time, she knew that as an officer of the law, Hank would be professionally obliged to alert the FBI if a fugitive was in their area. "Okay. I won't say a word. But I need you to know how hard that is for me."

"I know, I know," Claire said with a laugh. "Maybe I can meet with the poor kid, tell him what happened to his mother, and he'll disappear. Then I can tell the FBI the truth."

"You're not going to turn him in?" asked Margie.

Claire sat back, squinting her eyes. "I hadn't thought about it. You're right. Maybe I should. Depending on what his crime is, he could be dangerous." She set her mug down. "But still, I would like to talk to him. He deserves to know the truth."

Margie smiled. "Maybe you can find out his birthday, and see if it was before or after the accident."

Claire nodded. "Maybe."

They sat and chatted for another few hours until Margie was convinced that Claire was no longer on the verge of a nervous breakdown. She invited her to spend the night, but Claire insisted on going back to Orcas Island.

"I'm going to grab a few things from the cabin and go back to the hotel."

"How's everything going there?"

Claire shook her head. "Not great. The staff doesn't like me."

"Oh, I don't believe that! How can they not like you?"

"They can tell that I have no idea what I'm doing," Claire said. "Maybe they're right."

"No, maybe they're wrong," Margie countered. "You've come much too far to give in to bullying. You'll figure it out."

Claire smiled. "Thanks, Margie. I'll let you know what happens."

"Please do. I'll be up to visit soon."

Margie watched as her friend drove down the driveway and disappeared into the trees.

It was going to be a real struggle to not tell Hank. Hopefully she wouldn't have to keep quiet for long. The young man might make himself known, then Claire could explain the misunderstanding, and the FBI could talk to him about what they wanted. Easy as pie.

Hopefully.

Chapter Seven

There wasn't an easy way to get around the island, and Marty was far too paranoid to take a taxi. Plus, the public bus only ran during the summer. Not that he'd risk that, either.

It hadn't been much of a problem when he first got to Orcas Island. He'd caught a ride with a friendly driver from the ferry terminal to Moran State Park. From there, he was able to camp in the dense forest unnoticed. Though he was tempted to spend a few nights at a campsite, he resisted. If the FBI knew he was in the area, it was too risky.

It was his own fault if they found him, too. He got sloppy and used his burner phone to call his best friend – a number that the FBI was watching. He'd needed her help, though – in his rush, he had run out of his house without his wallet. Lesson learned.

Marty knew that he should leave the island. He knew he was playing with fire, but he just couldn't leave. Not yet. His mom had made no attempt to contact him, but he held a small hope that the mother who abandoned him all those years ago had simply missed his letter.

Or maybe she was scared? It was possible that the FBI had already gotten to her. They could be setting a trap for him...

He didn't care. After enduring four straight days and nights of heavy rain, Marty decided that he'd had enough. He would go to Claire's place and see what she had to say for herself.

It wasn't like he had a ton of options at this point. His own parents, his adoptive parents, were back in Spain. It's where his mother – er, his adoptive mother – had grown up, and he didn't want to tell them what was going on, worrying them from an ocean away.

Plus, he was still angry at them for hiding his adoption from him for all these years. If it hadn't been for his drunken aunt at Thanksgiving, Marty never would've found out the truth.

His mom, ever the free spirit, didn't understand why he got upset. "It's not like we were *lying* to you," his mom said, shaking her head, sending her long brown hair into violent waves. "We planned to tell you, but we wanted to wait until you were older, until you could understand."

"Yeah," his dad had added, nodding eagerly.

"So you waited until I was almost thirty?" Marty asked, incredulous.

"Of course not, but as you got older, you were such a moody teenager..." His mom trailed off and laughed. "What does it matter? What does it change? I'm still your mother, aren't I?"

It changed everything, of course, but Marty couldn't find the words for it. It felt like he'd been the butt of a thirty-year joke.

Had everyone known that he was adopted? Did they laugh about it behind his back?

His parents had hidden it from him for so long that it stood to reason they could've lied to him about everything else in his life. He'd believe anything, apparently. It seemed impossible for Marty to ever trust again.

"She was a very sad girl, nice, but very sad," his mom explained. "She didn't *want* to let you go. She lived with us for the last three months of her pregnancy, and a week after we adopted you, she disappeared."

It made no sense to him. The records surrounding his adoption were sealed, with no option to open them. His parents had a single picture of her, his birth mom, the one who went by Rebecca.

It was a fluke he'd even managed to find her. Marty debated for weeks whether it might be worth it to sign up for an ancestry website. The most popular one, with the most possible matches, had recently had a data breach. Thousands of people's information was hacked, and Marty would normally want nothing to do with a company like that.

Yet...the temptation of finding his birth mother was too great. He sent his DNA in and got a match. With the FBI chasing him down, though, he didn't have time to wait to see if she was interested in meeting. He took advantage of the ancestry website's security weakness, which had been fixed poorly, and got her name and address for himself. It was a bit of light hacking, but for a good cause – he was able to find out that his birth mother was now going by the name Claire.

From what he could see online, her life had been an interesting one. Despite giving him away, she'd had three daughters – none of whom she gave away – and recently bought an expensive hotel on the island.

It nagged at him. That was really what made him come all the way to Orcas Island. He needed to know. How could she leave him to some couple she met in a Kmart parking lot, but keep three other kids?

That was what he needed to know. He wanted to hear what this woman had to say for herself, what had been so wrong with him that she left him behind.

Naturally, he couldn't admit to himself that he wished she'd welcome him with open arms, tell him she'd made a mistake, and offer him a safe place to hide from the FBI.

That was too unlikely to even fantasize about. Unfortunately for Marty, he'd never realized how difficult it was to hide, especially when all of the people willing to hide him were under surveillance by the FBI.

He packed his tent before hiking out of the park and onto the main road. There was no sidewalk, and though it felt a bit precarious at times, most of the drivers moved relatively slowly. He kept the hood of his jacket up. To any passersby, he looked like another anonymous hiker.

It was too far and too windy to walk all the way to Claire's cabin, though, so when he got to Eastsound, he rented a kayak and launched it from the bay. It was an easy, peaceful trip out and around the western tip of the island – so peaceful that he almost forgot he was a fugitive for a few minutes.

After finding a suitable beach, he paddled in and dragged the kayak onto shore. From there, he made the trek to the main road, still going unnoticed, and to the address for Claire's place. He wasn't positive she was living there, but that was where her DNA results were supposed to go.

Marty may have broken a few rules getting that information from the system, but to be fair, the company's security was almost nonexistent.

When he got to Claire's road, he paused. It didn't seem like anyone was around, and it was starting to get dark. He figured he would take his chances and started to walk through the woods alongside the rocky driveway. When he reached the cabin, he waited for half an hour, looking for any signs of life inside.

There was nothing. No lights, no sounds, no movements. He stood there and debated what to do. His damp clothes clung to his skin and sent a chill through his core.

It didn't seem like he'd be meeting his birth mom today. However, it seemed like the perfect chance to get a hot shower, and to change into dry clothes.

He approached the cabin slowly, still listening, still hearing nothing. Marty managed to pop open a window in the back and pull himself inside.

As he walked around the tight space, he got a feel for the lady that was his mother. There wasn't much in there. She was living curiously simply, almost like he was, out in the woods.

It seemed like no one had been in the cabin in a long while. Though he wanted to poke around more, he decided to take a chance on showering. He was filthy and freezing, and it wouldn't take more than ten minutes.

Marty stepped into the bathroom and closed the door. He comforted himself with the thought that if she were to come home in the next ten minutes, he'd have to be one of the unluckiest guys alive.

Chapter Eight

T hank goodness for Margie. Claire felt ten times better. In the moments before Margie reeled her in, Claire felt like she was going to lose her mind.

Margie was right, as morbid as it was. If Becca's son wanted to harm her, he could've done it already. He knew where she lived, but instead of harming her, he tried to set up a meeting. In *public*. He just wanted to talk.

Probably.

Perhaps tomorrow, after a good night's sleep, she could give the FBI agents a call and clear things up. She'd show them the letter, and the picture, and then they'd all have a laugh about the misunderstanding.

She opened the door to her cabin and flopped onto the couch. Enough worrying for the day; what she really needed to do was focus on the papers that Chip had given her. He'd put a lot of time into organizing those numbers for her, and she desperately wanted to understand them.

There was a chance she'd run into him that evening at the hotel, so she'd look over the figures before she left for the night.

Claire picked up the pile of papers and focused her eyes on the first page. She was lost in thought when she heard a noise.

That was odd. It sounded like it was nearby. Claire paused, lowering the papers slowly.

She sat still, listening. It sounded like it was coming from the bathroom.

Claire let out a sigh. There was a small hole near the bathroom window. She'd been warned about it before she moved in, but she didn't think much of. It seemed too small for anything bigger than a bee to get through, yet somehow a chipmunk had gotten in last week.

It had been quite a scene. The poor little creature had run around, squeaking in terror, and Claire ran after it, in a similar panic. She'd had to open the door and chase it with a broom until it found its way out.

Why hadn't she plugged that hole when she had the chance? She was going to be smarter this time – she was going to give the chipmunk a clear exit. She quietly got up and crept over to the corner where she kept the broom. Then she tiptoed to the front door and opened it.

Bracing herself, she popped the bathroom door open.

And screamed.

The man in the bathroom screamed back.

"Please! It's okay," he said, hands up.

Claire backed up, clutching the broom in front of her like a baseball bat. She could hardly see his face. He was dressed in dark clothes and had a hood pulled over his head. "Stay there!"

He nodded, hands still up in the air.

She paused. "I'm going to call the police!"

"Please don't call the police," he said, taking a step forward.

Claire couldn't help it; she shrieked again. She had the urge to run away, but when he stepped into the light, she froze.

There was something familiar about him and she stared at him, trying to place it. Claire was transfixed by the man's eyes. They looked *exactly* like Rebecca's.

"I've been camping for a while, and I just wanted to shower. I was about to crawl back out of the window when you came back. I didn't think you were home..."

She lowered the broom a few inches. "Are you...the one who sent me that letter?"

"You got it?" A smile spread across his face. "I'm sorry. This isn't how I wanted to meet you. I'm Marty."

Claire felt like she was going to lose her balance. Rebecca had always said that she wanted to have a son named Marty, after Marty McFly in *Back to the Future*.

She'd loved those movies, raving about how she wanted to live in the Wild West with Doc Brown and never have to worry about rules again.

"Marty," she whispered.

He nodded, putting his hands down and lowering his hood.

"You look so much like her," Claire said, shaking her head.

He tilted his head to the side. "Like who?"

She couldn't stop staring. She cleared her throat. "Your mother."

His face contracted, frowning and encircled with lines. "I'm sorry... I thought you were Claire Cooke?"

The cold air blowing in from the front door was too much. She turned around and quickly shut the door.

Marty was still standing in the doorway of the bathroom. He didn't look threatening at all, with his wet hair and crystal clear green eyes, the exact shade of Rebecca's.

Really, the exact shade of Claire's as well, though she never spent much time looking in the mirror. She had, however, spent many hours of her life looking into Rebecca's eyes, overwhelmed with love or jealousy or exasperation. Until one day, she never got to look into them again.

"Do you want to sit down?" she offered, pointing to the couch. "Are you hungry?"

He slowly approached the couch and sat. "No, thank you. I'm fine."

No, thank you. How polite.

He spoke again. "I'm sorry, but do you know where my mother is? I was hoping to meet her."

She walked to the kitchen and filled the tea kettle before placing it on the stove. He didn't move, and Claire felt her muscles relaxing. She set the broom down.

"If your mother is who I think she is," Claire said slowly, "I'm very sorry, but she's no longer with us. She passed away years ago."

Brow again furrowed, Marty looked down. "Oh."

"I'm so sorry."

He looked up at her. "How is that possible? She just came up in that system and we were matched and –"

"It was me," Claire said gently. "I'm Claire Cooke. Your mom, Rebecca, was my twin sister."

He eyed her warily for a moment. "Twin?"

Claire nodded, rushing into the other room to dig through a pile of unpacked boxes. She pushed two out of the way, letting them fall to the floor with a boom.

Claire didn't care. She didn't even remember what was in those boxes. The only one she was interested in was labeled "bedroom closet." She never traveled far without these precious belongings, one of which was a photo album of her family.

She pulled it triumphantly from its place and placed it in Marty's hands. "That's us. On the cover. With our parents and our sister Holly."

Marty stared at the picture before silently opening the album.

Claire sat across from him and shifted nervously in her seat. Would this make him angry? Rebecca used to have such a temper.

"How did she die?" he asked softly.

Claire clasped her hands awkwardly in her lap. "A plane crash."

He flipped the pages and reached a section of newspaper clippings about the crash. "Your parents, too?"

Claire nodded. "Yes. And Holly, and her husband."

He sat back and looked up at her. His lips had faded to a pale pink.

"Can I get you some tea?" she asked, standing up.

He nodded, remaining silent as she futzed around the kitchen.

She returned a few minutes later with a mug for each of them.

"Thank you," he said, accepting it and taking a sip.

He looked so much like her, especially with the faces he was making. It made Claire feel sick, homesick almost, like Becca was looking back at her from the grave.

She spoke again. "I'm so very sorry, Marty. My sister was..." She released another unintentional sigh. "Troubled. She had issues, and we tried to help her, but it was difficult. She rejected help, she ran away. I didn't even know that she had a son."

He let out a sigh. "Yeah, well, I didn't know she existed until recently."

She sat quietly as he leafed through the album again. Finally, he looked up. "A few weeks ago, my parents told me about her. They said that they let a woman live with them for a few months. She was pregnant and..." He shook his head. "After I was born, she asked if they wanted to adopt me. So they did, and they hid it from me. Until now."

"I see." Claire's heart sank. He looked so sad. "Parents make mistakes sometimes."

He nodded, but said nothing.

Claire was fighting with two warring factions. On the one hand, she wanted to give Marty the time and space to absorb this news. On the other hand, she wanted to know everything about him and his life up to this moment.

She took a sip of tea and smiled.

He shut his eyes and shook his head. "You know, I couldn't understand why my mom would've abandoned me, and then turned around and had three other kids, but now it makes sense."

Oh, her heart. It felt like a knife went clean through. "That's not the case, not at all. My girls – I adopted them after Holly died."

She wanted to add, "I would've adopted you, too," but the words failed her.

Marty nodded. "I'm sorry. I didn't mean to scare you." He stood. "I just wanted to know about...I don't know. I thought it would mean something. I thought it would explain something."

Claire stood, too. She didn't want him to leave. Not yet. "I know I'm not who you were looking for." She stopped, trying to form her thoughts. "But we're still...family."

He paused, a flash of surprise crossing his face before breaking into a smile. Claire smiled back.

A moment later, a knock boomed through the front door.

Chapter Nine

That was oddly loud, as if the door was hollow. This cabin wasn't as solid as it looked.

There was no way she hadn't heard it, though, and there was no response. Chip stood there, guilt simmering in his chest, as he considered the fact that he may have run Claire off the island for good.

No one had seen her at the hotel for the rest of the day, and her car was still missing from the parking lot. He'd allowed his ego to take over, and he'd acted like an absolute jerk.

The door opened by a crack and Claire peeked out. "Oh, hi," she said.

She hadn't run off! "Hey!"

Claire stepped out of the doorway and looked behind him. "Is everything okay?"

"Yes, everything's great, nothing wrong at the hotel." He paused. Chip hadn't planned out exactly what he wanted to say, and now found himself feeling awkward and unbalanced. He cleared his throat. "I just came by to tell you that I'm really sorry for the way I behaved today."

"Oh." She tugged on the door and it clicked closed. "You know what, I'm sorry too. I've been so scattered today, and I had some unexpected news and –"

"I know, I heard."

Her eyes widened. "You did?"

"I didn't mean to eavesdrop," he rushed to add, "but when I walked in I heard you talking to – I think it was your daughter?"

Really smooth, Chip. Tell her you were listening in on her phone call. Just keep digging that hole deeper and deeper.

"Yes," she said slowly. "That was – she's okay, I don't normally take personal calls when I'm working. Like I said, it's just been a bit of an...unusual day."

Chip was relieved she didn't seem angry. "Of course! Well, I wanted to let you know that your next room is ready, and..." He took a breath. This was much harder than he'd expected.

How was it that he could go toe to toe with any executive, but this soft-spoken woman had him completely put out? "And I wanted to make it up to you. I'd like to take you to dinner."

She smiled. "Sure, yeah. That's nice of you. I'd like that."

"Okay." He took a step back. "There's an excellent seafood place just down the road. I know the owner and can get us a table."

Claire stared at him for a beat before answering. "You mean right now?"

She was going to think that he was hitting on her, and that wasn't his intention. He reached into his coat and removed a file with the hotel reports in it. "I have all of the papers from this morning, so we could talk about them there? I mean, we could talk about them here, too, if you prefer?"

"No, no," she laughed, glancing back at the door. "Seafood would be great. Let me grab my coat."

She flashed a smile and disappeared into the cabin.

He got the distinct feeling that he'd made her uncomfortable, but he couldn't narrow down one of the many reasons of why that might be. Chip stood there, mentally berating himself as he stared at the door.

It had been a long time since he'd felt like he didn't know what he was doing at work. He had been secure in his role at the hotel – until, that is, Steve had absconded and Claire had come along. Suddenly he felt thrown off, like he'd lost control. Perhaps that was another reason why he'd reacted to her so poorly.

Claire emerged from the cabin a minute later and accepted his offer for a ride to the restaurant. As she opened the passenger door for herself, he realized he could've done that for her.

Or maybe that would've made her feel even more uncomfortable? Now that he wanted to make up for being rude, he didn't know how much was too much.

"I hope you like seafood," he said cheerfully as he got into the driver's seat.

"Very much, yes."

"Great," he said, forcing a smile. He hadn't said the word "great" as many times in the last six months as he had in the last six minutes. He needed to pull it together.

It wasn't a long drive to the restaurant, and embarrassingly, the place was nearly empty when they got there. There was no need for Chip to brag about knowing the owner – the hostess seated them immediately at a table overlooking the water.

Claire sat down and pulled her phone from her purse before frowning.

"Is everything okay?" he asked.

She nodded quickly, throwing it back into her purse. "Yes, everything's fine. I just realized that my phone's dead again."

"Is it broken?" He shifted in his seat. It wouldn't be easy to replace it if so. Living on an island had many perks, but buying new electronics wasn't one of them.

"No, nothing like that," she said, shaking her head. "It's a silly thing, really, but it didn't charge last night."

He leaned forward. "You mean at the hotel? Did you lose power in your room?"

"No, it was –" She stopped herself. "I don't want to complain. I stayed in the Sunshine Suite, and it was lovely, and the view was wonderful, and...."

"Please," he said, trying to soften his voice. "I want to hear."

She waved a hand. "It's just that the electrical socket was loose, and I didn't notice, so the charger fell out. I marked it down as one of my potential improvements, which I now realize are silly."

"That's not silly." Chip shook his head. "Not at all. That's an easy fix, too."

She smiled.

Chip kept talking. "I can see if they have a charger here. If you're waiting on a call, I –"

"No, it's okay." Claire cleared her throat. "I'm sorry that I was so distracted earlier today. And I know that words don't mean much, but I'm not normally like this."

"Of course not," he said.

She smiled. "My goal was to give you my full attention, and from now on, I will."

Her graciousness only made him feel like more of a jerk. Chip had a reputation for being tough. Someone had to be, especially since Steve was overly kind to everyone. Chip wasn't afraid to enforce rules, or to be the bad guy.

Usually, it worked well, but this time, he'd gone too far.

"You are completely fine," he said. "I'm just – well, I don't come from a hospitality background either."

"It seems like you really care about the hotel," Claire said.

Her eyes were the prettiest shade of green. He had never seen eyes quite like hers before.

He nodded. "I do."

"I'm not going to pretend to know half as much as you do, but I also want it to succeed," she said. "I've been reading books, and I hired Ken, and I just want everyone to work well together."

"I agree with that. I think it's exciting that you hired an expert," he said, lying through his teeth.

Ken seemed like an idiot, and Chip had hoped that he'd never have to meet him. However, if his penance for the way he'd treated Claire was to tolerate this guy, he would do it.

The waitress stopped by and immediately started gushing about Claire's bracelets.

"Those bangles are stunning!" she said, gently touching the shining metal. "Where did you get them?"

Claire clasped her hands together and looked down admiringly at her wrist. "Thank you! They were made by an artist here on the island. I was over in Olga at that art store. Do you know the one?"

She nodded. "The Artworks, yeah. One of my friends sells her paintings there."

Claire was busy slipping one of the bracelets off of her wrist to hand to the waitress. "Her name is inscribed on the inside there. She's so talented."

The waitress studied the dainty, silver bracelet, as did Chip. It had tiny, intricate designs in the metal which blended into the hammered surface.

"Gah, I love it," the waitress said, handing it back to Claire.

Claire shook her head. "No, you keep it."

"Are you sure?" she asked, a look of surprise crossing her face.

Claire nodded. "Yes, please. I bought too many, as you can see."

"Well, thank you!" The waitress beamed, slipping the bracelet onto her wrist. "I'm sorry, I forgot to tell you the special for today."

Chip sat back, dazed by this interaction. Perhaps he had been outside of the feminine world for too long. It had been nearly two years since he broke up with his last girlfriend. Or rather, she had broken up with him.

Regardless, Claire's generosity was still unusual to him. There was no way that his ex-girlfriend would have given away a bracelet like that.

Or given away anything, for that matter.

"Oh, that does sound good," Claire said, looking at Chip.

He hadn't been listening, so he had to respond with, "Should we order it?"

She shrugged. "Sure."

They were treated to an appetizer of fresh clams, and at Claire's insistence, Chip talked through the aspects of his report. She listened intently as he discussed profit margins, lead time trends, group allocation, and other general principles of hotel revenue management.

Surprisingly, Claire was able to follow most of it, asking appropriate questions and clarifying terms she didn't know.

Chip could talk about this stuff all night, and forgetting himself, he practically did. Despite not wanting to bore her to death, he realized that the restaurant was closing as he was finishing the last few pages of the report.

"We should probably get going," Claire said with a nervous smile. "But we need to meet again to go over the rest of your ideas."

His face brightened. "That would be great."

Great. Again. Did he not know any other words?

"I need to go back to my cabin and grab a few things, but after that I'll be at the hotel. Maybe we can meet in the morning?"

He stood up, nodding. "Yes, sure."

Chip drove back to the cabin and dropped her off. He couldn't be sure if he was imagining it, but it seemed like she was in a rush to get out of the car.

He'd bored her enough for one night. She waved at him from the door and he took the hint, driving off and into the night.

Chapter Ten

How was it possible to spend months – years, even – living the same life, day after day with work, traffic, the grocery store, an occasional visit to the dentist, and in one day everything changes?

When Claire used to read memoirs about other people's exciting lives, or when she stared longingly at the exotic locations on her desk calendar, she thought that one day, if her life ever evolved away from her gray cubicle, she'd be ready for it. She'd enjoy it and embrace it, as she had the rest of her life.

Yet here she was, with more excitement in the last week than she'd had in perhaps the last ten years, and she had no idea how to handle it.

She'd regained a bit of calm during her dinner with Chip, but she decided that perhaps she wasn't cut out for an exciting life. The events of the day had left her walking around in a daze. What was she thinking, agreeing to go to dinner and leaving Marty alone in the cabin?

Or at least she hoped he was still in the cabin. Claire stood in the doorway, waving at Chip as he drove away. There was a chance she would open the door and Marty would be gone. Then she'd have to wonder if she'd imagined it all, like a fit of madness.

Once she was satisfied Chip had left, she carefully opened the door and called out, "Hello?"

"Hey," a voice called back.

Phew. She hadn't imagined it after all.

Marty popped his head out of the bedroom, a sheepish look on his face. "I'm sorry. I wanted to see if there were any more photo albums."

"Of course," Claire said, closing the door behind her. "You can help yourself. Or could you not find them?"

He shook his head. "I found them. I just put them back."

"Oh, good." She stood there, smiling at him, again struck by how much he reminded her of Becca. "I'm sorry about leaving like that. I think I panicked. I didn't want him to know that you were here, because of the..." Her voice trailed off.

"Because of what?"

She might as well say it. "Because of the FBI." She thrust a plastic bag into his hands. "Are you hungry? I saved most of my meal for you. It's probably not warm anymore, but it's quite good."

He set the bag on the coffee table. "The FBI talked to you?"

Claire nodded. "Yes."

His eyes darted around the room. "Do they know I'm here?"

Claire shook her head. "No, of course not. Unless they're spying on me."

He picked up his coat. "They might be. Have you texted anyone about me? Or made any calls?"

"No."

He zipped his jacket and picked up his backpack. "That's good. You should deny ever having met me."

He opened the front door and paused, looking back at her. "It was nice meeting you, Claire."

"Wait!" she said. "Don't go yet. I think it's safe. They came looking for you at the hotel, not here."

He raised an eyebrow. "Really? What did they say?"

"They didn't tell me much. They thought I was lying to them about never having a son."

He nodded, taking another step out the door.

"What is it that they want to talk to you about?" she asked. "Maybe we can clear things up with them?"

He smiled. "I wish it were that simple."

"Hang on." Claire picked up the to-go box. "You should at least eat something. If you don't want this, I can get you something else. I don't have much food here, but –"

"Thank you, I appreciate it," he said. "But I should go."

"Come on, sit down. At least for a minute. If the FBI knew that you were here, wouldn't they have caught you by now?"

He frowned. "Yeah..."

Marty seemed to debate this for a moment before finally closing the door and taking a seat on the couch.

Claire let out a sigh. She wasn't ready for him to run out of her life yet.

She busied herself with getting the leftovers onto a plate. In truth, she'd only taken one bite of her meal. She'd hoped that Marty would still be there when she got back, and purposely ordered something that would reheat well – a fisherman's pie.

Before he could protest any more, she popped the plate into the microwave and pulled two sodas from the fridge.

"It's a misunderstanding," he said taking a sip of the soda.

"What is?"

He cleared his throat. "With the FBI. I'm not dangerous or anything."

"Of course you're not," Claire said with a smile. She pulled the plate out of the microwave and set it on the small kitchen table.

"Did the FBI tell you why they wanted to talk to me?" he asked, standing up.

Claire shook her head. She was trying not to pry, even though she'd been hit with a second wave of urgently wanting to know everything about him. "They just accused me of lying. I had no idea what they were talking about."

He let out a sigh. "They've been led to believe that I was selling secrets to the Chinese government."

Claire couldn't help it; she laughed out loud. "That sounds like the plot of the bad spy movie."

He smiled, taking a bite of the pie. "You're telling me."

"Well, that's just silly! Can't you just tell them that you didn't do it?"

"It's hard. They have evidence that I did."

Claire took a seat across from him. "Like the evidence they had that I have a son?"

He offered a weak smile. "Yeah, kinda like that."

A weight lifted from Claire's shoulders. Though in her heart she didn't believe that Marty could possibly be a dangerous criminal, it was nice to have it confirmed. Even if it was just by him. "I had a hard time convincing them that I didn't have a son, so I can only imagine."

He set his fork down. "Yeah. It's...complicated."

"I'd love to hear about it," she said, smiling at him. "If you don't mind?"

He stared at her for a moment before continuing. "Okay, ah, I don't know where to start. I guess it began back in college. I went to school for engineering, but failed out."

Claire nodded. Lucy had followed a similar path, but she didn't think that it was the appropriate time to interject that fact.

Marty continued his story. "I was still friends with some of the guys, though, and after they graduated, they started a pet project called SureFired. It's basically a computer program that can help predict wildfires, and how best to fight them."

Claire raised her eyebrows. "Oh! How neat."

"It was," he said, becoming more animated. "SureFired was really cool. They asked me to help them with it, because I was good at coding – I mean, I'm still good at coding – and I was working at this dumb job as a security guard where I had a lot of free time. Anyway, I helped them get it off the ground and build a company around it."

"That's amazing!"

He smiled shyly. "It was, and it started to get a lot of attention. Before long, they had a crazy valuation – like, in the hundreds of millions – and an offer to sell the company."

Claire sat back. "Wow."

"I didn't think that we should sell, but I wasn't technically one of the founders, so I didn't get a say. I decided to stay on after the company sold, and after a year, we had almost two hundred people on staff. There was a little bit of everything from other programmers to environmental engineers to scientists. They helped us collect data and analyze previous fires."

"What exactly does SureFired do?" asked Claire.

"Oh, right, sorry. Using all this data, along with information about wind patterns, dryness, topography and stuff, we could predict how the fires would spread, and what areas were most vulnerable. It can tell firefighters where to work, and most importantly, it's supposed to give people a warning as to when they need to evacuate."

"That is so cool, Marty!"

"Thanks." He smiled. "After a while, I ended up getting promoted to manager."

A swell of pride grew in Claire's chest. "That's so impressive."

"Thank you." He let out a sigh. "The firm that bought us wasn't happy with our progress, though. We needed more time to make sure what we were doing made sense. We needed to test it with real fires and watch them play out. We definitely didn't have the capability to accurately warn people – not yet.

"But the new CEO didn't care. He secured a contract with the US government to sell them the technology, and he promised to have it ready for the wildfire season this year, this April. He said it would save money in firefighting, in damages, and in productivity, because people wouldn't evacuate needlessly. He completely oversold it."

Claire was familiar with the short-sighted policies that often occurred in large companies. "I see."

He took another bite of the meal, talking with his mouth full. "I mean, this was a huge deal, and they stood to lose millions. Once that deal was made public, a private equity firm swooped in and offered to buy the company for a billion dollars. So, of course, the CEO didn't want to hear that it wasn't ready. He didn't care if it would put firefighters and regular people in more danger than ever. I got into an argument with him and told him that if he didn't slow down, he was going to get people killed."

Claire was perched at the edge of her seat. "What did he say?"

"Nothing. The next thing I knew, I was accused of sending emails to China from my work account, trying to sell proprietary information from SureFired." He rubbed his face. "Like I even know who to sell it to, or that I'd be stupid enough to send things from my work email."

Claire frowned. "It sounds like it's easy enough to explain, though?"

"It's considered espionage, economic espionage. They think I'm selling trade secrets to a foreign government." He stared at his hands. "It's a serious charge. I didn't know what to do, so I ran."

Well. This wasn't something she could've come up with in her wildest dreams. "How long has it been?"

Marty looked up for a moment, thinking. "About six weeks."

"You missed Christmas?" she asked, heart sinking.

Marty laughed. "Yeah, I missed Christmas. My parents thought I went skiing with friends."

Claire sat back and studied him.

"Thank you again for this. It really was delicious." He took the last bite of food before taking his plate to the sink. "You know, I don't expect you to believe me."

Claire stood up, too. "I do believe you, and I want to help you."

His bright green eyes shined at her. "I – well, I can't tell you how much that means to me, Claire."

She beamed. She might not be cut out for an exciting life, and she might not know anything about hotel revenue management, but Claire had many years of experience as a mom.

Not that she was Marty's mom, of course. He had a mom – two, actually. It wasn't her role to fill, but right now, he needed *someone*.

Her own girls were off, living their lives, and it'd been some time since Claire felt like anyone really needed her. They were still family, after all.

"Good," she said. "We'll figure this out together."

Chapter Eleven

The anger Chip had felt toward Claire was now redirected where it belonged – at himself. He laid in bed that night, staring up at the ceiling and simmering in his thoughts. Self-loathing was nothing new to him, though it had been some time since he'd felt this angry at himself.

After moving to Orcas, he'd managed to make the right choices – most of the time. His history, however, held an unfortunate period where he was often full of anger and regret. It was an awful, perpetual state and Chip lived like that, muddled and confused, for many years.

He'd managed to snap out of it this time, though, and his dip into that old darkness was brief.

Chip now realized how silly it was for him to project the hotel's failings onto Claire. She'd only just gotten there. He was the one who'd been working there for years. It was his problem that he could never get Steve to listen, or that Steve never agreed to make the improvements the hotel needed.

Also, it'd been a tough few years for the hotel industry. As lovely as it was, even The Grand Madrona couldn't escape reality.

Miraculously, it seemed that his relationship with Claire wasn't ruined. She was far from the unreasonable villain he'd made her out to be, and he was humbled by her – by her grace and her kindness.

Now his biggest issue would be calming the unprofessional giddiness he felt when he thought of her. No need to make a fool of himself again.

He reported to his office early the next morning and managed to sort out two issues before the clock even struck nine.

The first had to do with housekeeping. They'd recently invested in a new program where the housekeepers could create their own schedule. It allowed for greater flexibility and less oversight, which Chip thought was great.

However, some of the staff still struggled with locking themselves out of the system every few days. Chip was the go-to for fixing that, as well as restoring the backup when the schedule kept being inexplicably deleted.

The second issue stemmed from a guest complaint. Chip found the gentleman at the front desk, suitcase in hand, gesticulating wildly at an immovable Gigi.

It took Chip almost ten minutes to figure out what the problem was – an accusation that the hotel had lost the man's reservation.

They had several rooms open, so it wasn't a true problem, but the man kept saying that this was a "sign of things to come" and that he'd like to be offered a complementary night or two to make up for the inconvenience.

When the guest couldn't remember what type of suite he'd booked, Chip followed a hunch and called around to the other resorts on Orcas Island. He quickly found the man's reservation at Rosario Resort, down the road. It was a lovely place, but it wasn't the Grand Madrona.

The would-be guest sheepishly thanked Chip for his help and escaped to his car without another word.

Chip then breezed into the Plum Spoon to discuss next month's specials with the chef. On his way out, he caught sight of Claire and waved.

Her face brightened into a smile when she saw him. Almost immediately, the man next to her grabbed her elbow and turned her around, calling her attention to the far side of the room.

As Chip approached them, he heard the man say, "The windows are the eyes to the soul, and therefore, the souls to the room. Don't you see?"

Claire bit her lip. "Ah, yes."

"Good morning," Chip announced from behind them.

Claire spun around. "Hi! Chip, this is Ken Gallon. Ken, Chip is my general manager and revenue manager."

Ken looked him up and down, nodding. "It's a pleasure."

"Nice to meet you," Chip replied. He decided against offering a handshake, mostly because Ken's arms remained firmly crossed.

"How unusual for one person to be both the general manager *and* the revenue manager," Ken said. "What kind of struggle do you find in your role?"

What kind of struggle did he find? Was that a phrase from one of his hospitality books?

Chip frowned, but stopped himself from responding brusquely. He was far more familiar with Ken's type – a snob – than he was with Claire's. He still didn't quite know who Claire was.

"I wouldn't say I have any struggle at all," Chip said. "I've grown into both roles over the last ten years here."

"Oh, how nice." Ken smiled briefly, his nose scrunching like a rabbit.

Claire cleared her throat. "Are you free today, Chip? I thought we could all talk through some ideas."

"I would *die* for some coffee right now," Ken said, clapping his hands together. "Join us, Chip."

He shrugged. "Works for me."

The restaurant was nearly empty, and they took a table next to one of the largest "souls" in the room. Dan took Claire and Chip's orders before finding himself under interrogation with Ken.

"What sort of creamer options do you have?"

Dan tapped his pen on his notepad. "Well, we carry half-and-half, whole milk, skim – "

Ken waved a hand. "I mean what *else?*"

"We also have almond milk and soy milk."

"Hm." Ken drummed his fingers on his chin. "Thank you. Is it organic?"

Dan looked up. "I think so?"

"That's interesting." Ken stared at him. "I'll take my coffee with a dab of skim and a pack of Splenda. Just *one* Splenda, mind you."

Dan nodded. "Coming right up."

Ken waited until Dan left before speaking again. "You know, a lot of the luxury customers are going to expect their favorite creamer option to be readily available. Something to think about."

"What are we missing?" Chip asked, tilting his head. "Vanilla ice cream?"

"Oh, that'd be so good," Claire said with a smile.

Ken ignored her. "There are many more options, but that was a suitable list. For now. If we're going to try to get this hotel up to a four-star level, there is no detail too small."

Chip leaned forward. "Hang on. What is this about becoming a four-star hotel?"

"It's one of Ken's ideas," Claire said brightly. "He says it's a way to set us apart from other hotels and resorts on the island."

"Exactly, Claire." Ken winked at her. "But it's going to take a lot of hard work and dedication. Not that we're afraid of that, are we?"

Chip sat back and smiled. "What kind of hard work?"

"Where to start?" Ken let out a sigh. "We need to hire bellhops and offer full-service luggage handling. Then we should have valet parking, twenty-four hour room service, perhaps even a turndown service."

"Interesting." Chip crossed his arms. "What definition of four-star are you using? Who's going to accredit us?"

"Hold on there, partner," Ken said with a quick laugh. "We need to put all of these changes in place first, and then we can talk about accreditation."

Chip said nothing. That was a test, and Ken had failed. Despite the wide use of the star system for hotels, there was no standard for what the stars meant.

Plus, there was no accrediting body. Hotels made up their own star ratings and used whatever they felt fit best. There were some general ideas of what a four-star hotel should have, of course, but it was essentially meaningless.

Even ignoring all of this, Ken's thinking was way off. Guests didn't pay attention to stars nowadays. They cared more about reviews and ratings other guests left online.

Chip knew all of this because he researched it extensively. For years, he had offered discounts and free meals to their guests for completing surveys. That information was invaluable as to how to improve stays and attract more guests.

It was clear to Chip that while Ken talked a big game, he was making everything up as he went along.

"That's a lot to think about," Claire said. "Right now we have a staff of twelve people, and –"

Ken cut her off. "Now Claire, I've told you again and again. You're either committed to this process or you're not. You need to put the right energy into this world, and then you'll get the right energy back."

She stared at him and nodded. "Right. Okay."

Ken continued. "Since we're thinking of good energy, then this is as good a time as any to talk about some of the upcoming events at the hotel."

Dan stopped by with their coffees, silently dropping them off. Claire sat up straighter, apparently eager to hear what Chip had to say.

Chip watched them both closely, He couldn't help but notice that Ken made a face after taking his first sip of coffee.

Chip suppressed a smile and said, "We have a few annual events. Our next one is the Valentine's Day dinner."

"Excellent. Now is that a six or seven-course dinner?" asked Ken.

"Neither," Chip said slowly. "It's four courses. Guests choose an appetizer, an entrée, a dessert, and then a selection of cheeses, all paired with local wines and cider."

Ken frowned. "You know, if we're going to go for the four-star designation, you'll have to kick that up a notch."

"Noted." Chip set his coffee down. "After that, we have our Easter egg hunt on the grounds."

Claire smiled. "Oh, how sweet!"

Chip kept talking before Ken could make another comment. "Something new we'll be adding this year is the summer Fruit Festival."

"I think I've heard of that," Claire said.

Chip smiled at her. "You might have. It used to be held at an orchard on the other side of the island. Every year it got bigger and bigger, and last year the owner asked Steve if we could start hosting it."

"How neat!" said Claire. "How many people attend?"

"Last year there were almost five hundred."

"For a festival of *fruit*?" Ken asked, spitting out the word as if it were rotten.

Chip nodded. "Yes. Orcas Island used to have hundreds of acres of orchards. It was a major industry for the first settlers."

Claire leaned in. "Really?"

"Yep. It was all fruit, fishing, and logging." Chip liked that Claire seemed genuinely interested in this. He made a mental note to give her one of his Orcas Island history books later. "It wasn't until they figured out irrigation on the mainland that farming sort of fell by the wayside, and tourism became the major industry. The event combines the old and the new."

Claire smiled. "I love that. What kind of attractions are there?"

Chip looked around the table, relishing how unhappy Ken looked. "Well, there is a jam and preserve competition, of course. A pie baking contest, a pie eating contest – "

"Okay, that's enough," Ken said, putting up a hand. "Do we really want our hotel to be associated with a pie eating contest?"

For the first time during this conversation, Chip felt his temper flare. He decided to hold his tongue rather than respond to the "our hotel" comment.

"I think it's nice," Claire said. "What's wrong with a pie eating contest?"

Ken made a face that showed there was something very wrong with a pie eating contest. "If you want history, why don't you have something like...a Thanksgiving reenactment, later in the year?"

"What would that entail?" asked Chip.

Ken waved a hand. "You know, dress up half of the town children in pilgrim costumes and the other half in feathers. One could be the turkey. I know a company that designs magnificent sets. We can order one. *That's* the sort of aesthetic you want to go for. Not people shoving pie into their faces."

Chip cocked his head to the side. "Should I send a boat to the reservation and pick up some native actors for you?"

"Oh my gosh," Ken darted a hand to his mouth. "There's a reservation nearby? Even better!"

Chip nodded. "Yes, the Lummi tribe. My grandmother grew up there."

Ken let out a laugh. "Don't get your feathers ruffled, Chip. It's just an idea. This is all about ideas."

Chip raised an eyebrow. Luckily, he had no issues holding his temper this time. Not that Ken needed to know that. "My feathers?"

"Oh my goodness, I didn't mean it that way," Ken added, rushing to pat him on the shoulder. "You can't take it the wrong way."

Chip stared at him for a beat before cracking a smile. "I'm just pulling your leg." He stood up, pleased with the effect that he'd had. "I've got a couple of things to take care of, but maybe we can meet later, Claire?"

She nodded. "Sure, any time."

Chip walked off, smiling to himself.

Chapter Twelve

Ken set his coffee cup down and dabbed the corners of his mouth with a napkin. "You can't let him bully you, Claire. Remember, *you* are the one with a vision for this place."

Claire glanced at him before standing up. "Excuse me. I need to speak with Chip."

"It's just as well," Ken said with a sigh. "I've got to run. Until later. Don't forget – positive energy!"

Claire nodded at him. "Yes, right."

She went after Chip. He was already halfway to his office by the time she caught up to him.

"Hey!" she called out.

He spun around, a half-smile on his face. He didn't look angry.

That was good.

"What's up?" he asked.

Claire let out a breath. "I am so sorry about Ken. I'm not on board with that Thanksgiving idea. My daughter Lucy educated me long ago on the history of Native Americans and how –"

"Please. It's okay." He put his hands in his pockets. "I expected as much from Ken. He's my competition."

Claire cocked her head to the side. "Your competition?"

Chip nodded. "Yeah. I have to win you over to the dark side – to the side of the Fruit Festival."

She laughed. "It won't be that hard."

"Don't make up your mind yet," he said, putting his hands up. "I was thinking we could make a trip to one of the orchards. You should try some of the local ciders before giving the festival the axe."

Claire didn't need to be convinced. Regardless of Ken's opinion, she liked the sound of the Fruit Festival. It was a tradition. Who was she to tamper with tradition?

However, in her ploy to hide Marty, she needed to act as natural as possible. Spending time with her general manager fit the bill. "That sounds nice."

"Great. I'm free tonight," he said.

Claire had planned to spend the weekend at the cabin, getting to know Marty. "Ah. I'm not. What about next week?"

"Sure. Next Friday, then?"

She nodded. "Yeah, that's perfect."

"I can pick you up, if you'd like."

Oh dear. She didn't want anyone near the cabin. "How about I meet you there? I'm spending next week with housekeeping, and that'll just make it easier."

"That works." He pulled out his phone. "I'm sending you the address. See you at...?"

"Seven?" she suggested.

He nodded. "Seven's great. Good luck with housekeeping."

He walked off and Claire let out a sigh, releasing the tension in her shoulders. It was good that Chip wasn't upset...and that Ken had taken off for the day.

She'd thought Ken would have interesting ideas for the hotel, but so far he hadn't given her many specifics. In fact, the more she thought about it, the most specific he'd gotten was when he insulted Chip and criticized the Fruit Festival.

In her eyes, pies were exactly what this hotel needed. Claire saw The Grand Madrona as a family-friendly refuge, not a luxury resort. The fact that the hotel was elegant didn't mean that it could only cater to aristocrats.

She'd have to put her foot down with Ken, but there wasn't anything more to do on that subject now. Claire was spending the day with Gigi, learning how to take calls and book rooms.

The day flew by, surprisingly, because Gigi was happy to let Claire do most of the work. It was a great learning experience, and though Claire was sad to leave the hotel for the weekend, she was excited to have an excuse to spend time with her newly discovered nephew.

Taking a few days away from the hotel proved to be a wise choice. Claire loved having the time to get to know Marty as they spent hours talking, laughing, and cooking. They watched movies – Marty chose *Interstellar*, while Claire's choice was *Star Wars* – and Claire got to hear more about Marty's life growing up.

Though she didn't find any solutions to Marty's legal problem, Claire suggested that they hire an attorney who specialized in espionage. Marty was hesitant to agree; it seemed like he wished the problem would sort itself out.

Her argument was that while it'd be nice if the FBI figured out they were wrong on their own, it seemed unlikely. By Sunday evening, Marty acknowledged she was right, and he agreed they needed to find an attorney.

First thing Monday morning, Claire left a message for an old coworker, asking for a call back. Then, refreshed and full of hope, she returned to the hotel for her week of housekeeping duty.

She started her day in the employee locker room. Rhonda had left her a housekeeping uniform, and Claire beamed when she saw it. She fully planned on getting her hands dirty and learning first-hand how she could help make the housekeeping team's lives easier.

Luckily for Claire, the housekeepers were not shy about telling her what they needed. As Claire scrubbed toilets, flipped mattresses, and hauled trash, they told her about all of the improvements they'd like to see.

"Go ahead, try to push this vacuum," Layla, one of the youngest housekeepers, said to her on Tuesday.

Claire obliged, barely able to move the heavy thing along the carpet, its wheels squeaking.

"Oh yeah, that's awful," Claire said. "What's with the bag on here? It's so hard to get on."

"I know!" Layla said. "I think this vacuum is older than I am."

Claire laughed. All in all, the housekeepers' requests were entirely reasonable. They wanted new vacuums for each team, and a spare in case of breakdowns. They asked for new carts, and to have shampoo and conditioner dispensers installed in the showers.

That was Layla's idea – she despaired at all of the plastic that was wasted with tiny bottles in each room.

"I think we can do that," said Claire, writing their suggestions in her notebook.

The one request that would be harder to accommodate was a new hire. They explained to Claire how helpful it would be to have a part-time housekeeper to help pick up shifts during the busy season, or to cover when someone was off.

Claire thought this was reasonable, too, but was honest with them about needing to meet with Chip and seeing what the budget would allow.

They were satisfied with her response, and she set an appointment on her calendar to meet with them again in a month to make sure their suggestions were implemented to their liking.

The week went well, but by Friday, Claire was ready for a break. Housekeeping was hard work! She admired her staff – they didn't cut corners, and really, they weren't asking for much. Even so, she was nervous about bringing up the improvements to Chip. The man was intimidating.

Claire tried to remind herself that she was the boss, not him, but it was no use. Whenever she saw him, even just passing by, her stomach tightened.

It didn't help that he was so handsome. Maybe that was most of it? He was tall and had those broad shoulders, and he didn't dress like a manager, in suits and ties and things. He wore sweaters, usually, which somehow added to his ever-present confidence. Also, he had this great head of hair – jet black, with grays peppered in.

Her last boyfriend was bald, not that there was anything wrong with bald men. He had been cute, too. The only thing wrong with him was that he didn't want to be with someone who had kids. It took him almost two years to figure that out, though, and to break up with Claire.

When she finished for the day, Chip was nowhere to be seen. She decided to wait until their evening out to discuss the changes. She took a quick shower in the employee locker room before returning to the cabin.

Marty, bless his heart, had made dinner for them both – pan-fried salmon with asparagus.

"This is so nice!" she said as she walked in. He was too much. He'd spent the week cleaning the cabin, too, giving it the deep scrub it desperately needed.

"I feel guilty sitting around all day and eating your food," he said, setting the plates onto the little table. "I have to earn my keep somehow."

"Please, you should be relaxing. You were living in the wilderness for weeks!" Claire sat and watched him as he dashed around the kitchen. So much about Marty reminded her of Becca. It was the small things, the things she didn't even think about anymore – the quick way Becca used to move, or the scowl that would settle on her face when she was thinking.

Marty was like an echo of her. It dredged up old feelings and gave Claire a strong impulse to protect him – the way she never could protect her sister.

"I've also got a mixed rice going. I hope it's okay that I made it?" he asked, pulling her from her thoughts.

She smiled and nodded. "Of course! I got all of that food for you. I eat most of my meals at the hotel these days."

He stirred the pot. "How's everything going there?"

Claire shrugged. "Pretty good. No more visits from the FBI, at least."

He let out a laugh. "That's good."

"Have I told you about my friend Margie? She lives on San Juan Island. Her brother was in the FBI, so maybe he could help?"

"I appreciate the thought, but it won't work." Marty turned around to face her. "I have to get evidence before I can talk to them."

"What if that's not possible?"

He let out a sigh. "It'll be a lot less possible to prove anything if I'm behind bars."

Oof. Claire knew he was right, but it was still hard to think about. "Fair enough. Is the venture capital company going forward with buying SureFired?"

"As far as I know, yes." He rubbed his forehead. "I never thought that working on something so cool could go so wrong. People could lose their lives."

The timer dinged. Marty turned the oven off and brought the pot of rice to the table.

"How much rice would you like?" he asked, putting a heaping spoon onto her plate.

"That's good, thanks," Claire said.

He nodded, then served rice for himself before taking a seat. "It's wild. I don't think anyone else realizes how dangerous it'll be if the model misrepresents how much time people have to escape."

Claire looked up at him. "No pressure, huh?"

"Yeah, exactly." Marty took his seat. "Thanks again for letting me crash here. It's given me some time to think."

"I'm glad I could help," Claire said, smiling at him before taking her first bite of salmon. "Hey, this is pretty good, Marty!"

"Thanks! Yeah, it turned out okay."

Claire smiled to herself. What a scene this was. Sitting and having dinner with Becca's son. If only her mom and dad were still alive. They would've loved to meet him.

"Are you going back to the hotel tonight?" Marty asked.

"I wasn't planning to. I have a, uh, thing at seven."

Marty raised an eyebrow. "What kind of thing?"

Claire didn't know why she'd said it like that. Maybe because she felt inexplicably excited to spend more time with Chip, even if he did intimidate her. "It's a work thing, really.

The general manager of the hotel, Chip, wants to meet and discuss one of the summer events. A festival."

"Oh. Cool." Marty seemed to be studying her for a second. "Why do you look so worried?"

Claire laughed. He had his mother's keen intuition. "It's just a little strange, getting to know people here."

"Why?"

She set her fork down. She'd had this thought circulating in her mind, and it was too strong to keep ignoring. "Well, if Chip tells me about his life, then I have to share information about mine."

"Ah." Marty sat back and crossed his arms. "I mean, you probably shouldn't tell him about me, but I guess that's your choice."

Claire sputtered out a laugh. "No, obviously I won't talk about you. Not yet. It's everything else, actually."

"Like what?"

"Well," Claire said slowly, "when you were hacking my computer, did you see anything about how I bought the hotel?"

Marty took a bite of rice and answered, mouth full. "I didn't hack your computer. I only tapped into the DNA website's database to find your name and address. The rest of the information I got about you was on Facebook."

Claire frowned. Lucy was always scolding her about over-sharing online. "Really?"

He laughed. "Yeah, I didn't want to violate your privacy. Er, sorry. I guess I still kind of did."

She shook her head. "No, not at all. I'm glad that you're here."

"What's up with the hotel?"

"It's not the hotel, exactly. But if Chip wants to know about my life – that is, my old life – he's going to think it's pretty strange that a woman who worked as a paralegal was able to put down a few million dollars for a hotel."

Marty's jaw dropped. "A few *million* dollars? I didn't know paralegals made that kind of money."

Claire laughed again, shaking her head. "They don't, and we never had money. Ever. I over drafted my account more times than I'd like to admit." She felt strange telling him about the money. She'd assumed that he knew. Apparently, Marty hadn't snooped on her. It only made her like him more.

She continued. "It's a long story, but this is your family, too, and you deserve to know."

Marty sat back and focused his eyes on her.

She took a deep breath. "After the accident, I took the girls in, as you know. I was the only one who could do it, even though I was quite young. My brother-in-law Robert had an uncle – the guy he was named after, actually. He was supportive of me and the girls, of course, but couldn't help much. He was a younger guy, living the bachelor life, running a small business, and was a bit wild."

"And you weren't?" Marty asked.

"Ha! Not at all." Claire shook her head. "I spent all of my time in the library, studying."

"To be a lawyer, right?"

Claire smiled. "Right. Anyway, Uncle Robert started his own family a few years after the accident, and after some time, his business took off. He got sick last year and – well, his kids weren't helpful at all. He was heartbroken by how spoiled they'd become. He'd given them everything and more when they were growing up, and on his sickbed, he realized he'd spoiled them rotten."

"What happened to him?" asked Marty.

"He passed away." She took a sip of water. "Before he did, though, he asked me to come and visit. I didn't realize how ill he was, and I didn't take him too seriously when he talked about how angry he was with his children. He admitted he was, in a way, jealous of how well I'd raised the girls."

Marty frowned. "That's heavy."

"You're telling me." She shook her head. "So yes, he said he was a little jealous, but mostly proud of the girls. He told me he would leave a chunk of his fortune to his wife, the business to his kids – so they could learn the value of work – and the rest of his fortune to me."

"You didn't believe him?" Marty asked, leaning in.

"Not at all! I was sure he'd get better. I thought it was just bluster." She let out a sigh. "I wish you could've met him. He was a blast."

"Sounds like it."

She took another bite of food. "He made me promise not to tell anyone, but it's getting difficult. The girls have been asking questions, and I've decided they should know the truth."

"And me too?"

She nodded. "Yes, and you. Everyone else though...I'm not so sure. I thought that if I didn't tell anyone about my history, they could make their own assumptions."

"I think you should tell Chip," Marty said with a shrug.

"You do?"

He nodded. "He already knows that you have a bunch of money, so what's the harm?"

Claire frowned. That was an interesting point, but what if Chip only took it as further evidence that she had no business owning a hotel?

No, Marty was right. There was no point lying to Chip, especially if she sincerely wanted to get to know him.

"All right, I'll take your advice. This time."

Marty nodded, not looking up from his plate. "If my advice steers you wrong, you can hand me over to the FBI."

She laughed again. This kid was something else. "Great idea."

Chapter Thirteen

Maybe the tie was too much. Chip tugged at it, cursing himself. The cologne, too. Why was it seeping off him in such a sickening way? He'd only done two puffs, hoping to freshen up for his meeting with Claire.

It was the wrong way to go about things, it seemed. He now felt – and smelled – like a sleazy salesman. A sleazy fruit salesman.

Terrific.

He got to the orchard early, which was good, because it took fifteen minutes to get a table. Claire walked in precisely at seven o'clock and he stood, waving at her.

"Hi!" she said as she walked over.

She looked enchanting, causing him to lose his train of thought for a moment. Her dark hair was pulled back with some sort of a sparkly clip, and when she took her coat off, he had to force himself not to stare.

He didn't remember exactly what she'd worn that morning, but it wasn't this. At first he thought it was a sweater, but then he realized it was actually a dress. Whatever it was, she looked pretty, and much more comfortable than he did.

"This is exciting," she said, taking a seat.

"Yeah, it's a great place." He handed her a menu. "Are you hungry? The food here is good, too."

Claire shook her head. "Not really, I already had dinner. Sorry. I thought we were just getting cider."

"No problem," he said. "I'm sure you were hungry after Rhonda put you to work."

Claire laughed. "I was, but we had a nice time. And now I have a whole new section on my list of improvements."

"Ah, yes." Chip smiled. "A list of demands from housekeeping."

"It's not that bad," Claire said.

"Yeah?"

She put the menu in front of her face, leaving only her eyes peeking out. "Do you want to hear it now?"

"Sure. Why not?"

Claire ducked behind the menu. "All right, so they'd like new carts, new vacuums, an unscented cleaning product option, and dispensers in the showers."

He crossed his arms. "Why didn't they ask me for any of this stuff? I would've gotten it for them."

Claire's face reappeared, a small smile dancing on her lips. "I think they may be afraid of you."

"Afraid of *me*? Why?"

She set her menu down. "You're the boss. Everyone's afraid of the boss."

He scoffed, shaking his head. Was she wearing lipstick? She looked so nice...

"Especially when the boss is you," she added with a smile.

He didn't know what that was supposed to mean. Chip leaned forward. "Are you afraid of me?"

"Of course," she said without missing a beat.

Chip laughed. "Oh, c'mon."

She looked up at him with those green eyes, but said nothing.

He sat back. "Well then, I'm sorry I scared you."

"Don't be. It's easily done," she said. "I'm glad that we can get to know each other now."

Chip nodded. "Me too."

After they placed their orders, Claire set her gaze on him again. "I was hoping you could tell me more about your family, and about Lummi history?"

He smiled. "Of course. I brought a book about the history of Orcas Island for you, but I have other books about the tribes of the area, too."

"I would love to read them."

It seemed like she meant it. If she was willing to clean toilets all day for a week, then she likely was being genuine about reading a book.

"All right, where to start?" He paused. "Like I told Ken, my grandmother was a member of the Lummi tribe. She grew up on the reservation."

"Is it on the island?"

"No, it's on the mainland, near Bellingham."

Claire nodded and Chip kept talking. "She ended up having to go to public school, and that's where she met my grandfather. He wasn't native. He was an Irish Catholic boy.

Her parents didn't approve, but what can you do? They were in love, and no one could stop them."

"How romantic," Claire said.

Chip smiled. "Yeah, they were two of the best people I've ever known."

"Do you still have family living on the reservation?"

He shook his head. "No. I haven't been back in years, but when I was growing up, my grandma thought it was important to teach us our heritage – me and my brother. He was never really into it. He was older, you know, and wanted to live his own life, but I would go up to the reservation with her and visit her old friends. I learned a lot in those years."

Their drinks arrived, and Claire's stare remained unbroken. "That is so cool."

Chip shifted in his chair. After his grandmother had passed away, he'd made no effort to keep the connection, to keep going back and learning. He was ashamed of that, and it made him feel like he had no right to talk about his heritage.

Yet Claire seemed so enthralled that the guilt temporarily lifted.

"I read a bit about the history of Orcas Island," Claire said, "but there wasn't much about the native people. I thought that was so strange. The most they said was settlers brought diseases that killed a lot of the people here."

Chip nodded. "That's true, but there were still people and many tribes."

"Of course." Claire took a sip of her drink. "Did the Lummi live on Orcas Island?"

"Not all the time, no," he said. "Before the colonists arrived, tribe members migrated all over the coast. They came to the islands seasonally, following the salmon, and to pick fruit."

"Fruit again!" Claire said. "We should have something at the Fruit Festival about the native tribes."

He hadn't thought of that. "That would be nice."

"Did you know," she said, smiling broadly, "that Orcas Island wasn't named after the Orcas that live in the waters here?"

Of course he knew that, but she looked so excited that he hated to kill her fun. "Really?"

A broad smile crossed her face. "I'm sure you've heard this."

He shrugged, and she went on. "Okay, so, it was actually named after a Spanish military officer who explored the islands."

He tried to look surprised. "Oh yeah?"

"Yes, Juan Vicente de Güemes Padilla Horcasitas."

Now he was surprised. That wasn't an easy name to remember. "Wow."

"They shortened 'Horcasitas' to Orcas. Isn't that fun?"

He smiled. "Very."

Claire cleared her throat. "I'm sorry. I didn't mean to interrupt. Did you grow up around here?"

He shook his head. "Not exactly, but my son ended up going to college in Bellingham and I sort of tagged along."

"I bet he loved that."

Chip laughed. "I wanted to be close. Ah..." He paused. "It's a long story, but we were living in New York City at the time. My wife and I were going through a divorce, and I lost my job, and...yeah. Things sort of fell apart."

Claire raised her eyebrows. "Oh. I'm sorry."

He shook his head. "It's all right. It was all my doing. I've always been the master of my own destruction. Honestly, I was lucky Steve agreed to hire me on."

"Did you work in a hotel in New York?"

Chip shook his head. "No, not at all. I worked at an investment bank. Before the crash."

"Ah, I see," Claire said, slowly taking another drink from her bell-shaped glass. "So you caused the economy to crash?"

She was joking, but since he didn't know how to tell her the truth, he just laughed.

Claire clasped her hands in front of her. "You were right, by the way."

"About what?" he asked.

"This cider. It's delicious. We have to have it at the festival."

"Ah." He took a sip of his – he'd barely had any. He was talking too much. "I'll have to break it to Ken that I've won this battle."

Claire laughed and agreed.

"How about you?" he asked. "What did you do before you were buying hotels?"

She intertwined her fingers and tucked her hands under the table. "I was a paralegal."

"That's quite a jump."

She nodded. "You know, if I tell you how I ended up here, you might not believe me."

Chip laughed. "I'll be the judge of that."

She let out a sigh, took another sip of cider, and began. "Twenty-nine years ago, I was in my second year of law school, so sure that I had life figured out."

He nodded. "As we all do when we're twenty-two."

She cracked a smile. "I came home for spring break to a crisis. My twin sister Becca was in trouble, again, and my parents were going to rescue her."

Chip leaned in. It was loud in the tasting room and he didn't want to miss any details.

Claire continued. "They'd paid for her to stay at a rehabilitation center in Colorado."

He cocked his head to the side. "Was she an athlete?"

"No, it wasn't that kind of rehabilitation. Drugs, alcohol.... Becca was troubled." Claire paused. "Anyway, she threatened to leave and never speak to any of us again unless they came to get her. My parents panicked, as they always did, and my brother-in-law, who was a pilot, borrowed a little plane from a friend. He flew down there with my mom, my dad, and my older sister Holly. They picked Becca up," she said slowly, "and then crashed into a mountain."

Chip felt like he'd just crashed into a mountain, too. "I'm sorry, *what?*"

"No, I'm sorry," she flashed a pained smile. "I don't often tell this story anymore because everyone back home, you know, knew it already." She softened her voice. "There were no survivors."

Chip felt like his chair had shifted beneath him. "Wow, Claire, I'm so sorry."

"It's okay, it's been a long time." She let out a breath. "I left law school and adopted my sister's three daughters – my girls, Lucy, Lillian, and Rose." Claire smiled and pulled out her cell phone. "Here's a picture of us from a few months ago."

They looked like Claire, happy and smiling. He wanted to say that they were beautiful, like her, but it felt too awkward. "That's...unbelievable. I mean, I do believe you. I'm not trying to scare you again."

She laughed. "I know, and it gets crazier." She bit her lip. "Last year, my brother-in-law's uncle passed away, and it changed everything."

Chip frowned. "More than the plane crash?"

She looked around the room. "I mean, financially. I went from driving a fifteen-year-old car to buying the hotel."

"Wow." Chip realized that his mouth was hanging open. "You weren't kidding about having a wild story."

She laughed. "To be honest, I didn't want anyone at the hotel to know, because I didn't want them to think that I didn't know what I was doing. But you already know that I don't know what I'm doing, so there you go. That's the truth."

"This is great, Claire." Chip shook his head. It felt like she'd just thrown a pie in his face. He started laughing. "You know what? You're great."

She laughed. "Don't tease."

He shook his head. "I'm not. Do I seem like a guy who would tease his boss?"

Claire paused before responding. "Yes."

Chip laughed. "Well, I'm not, and I'm buying another round. On me."

"I can afford my drinks," she said.

He flagged down the waitress. "I don't care how many uncles you have. This is my island and here, I buy the cider."

She laughed, and Chip knew it was over for him. He'd do anything – absolutely anything – to keep hearing that laugh.

Chapter Fourteen

They were having so much fun that Claire completely lost track of time. Her initial plan had been to get back to the cabin after an hour, maybe an hour and a half, if service was slow.

Yet Chip kept her captivated the entire evening. He told her about the history of Orcas Island and the Lummi tribe, and they pored over the black and white photos in the book he'd brought along.

It wasn't just the island's past that he was interested in – he was interested in her past, too. It wasn't even that he was interested in hearing more about the money. He didn't seem to care about that at all.

Perhaps Marty was right. Chip already knew that she was "rich," even if Claire didn't think of herself that way, and the truth of where it came from didn't matter.

Chip was more focused on her transformation into an orphan and a mom of three all at once. He asked her about the jobs she'd held, and loved her stories from working in the public defender's office. He loved hearing about her friendship with Margie and the antics their girls had gotten themselves into over the years.

He even slipped in a clumsy question about her dating life, asking if the girls had a stepdad of sorts. She told him no, and that her last boyfriend broke things off because he couldn't see himself as a father, even to older children.

Claire wasn't sure if she imagined it, but he seemed relieved by this. Though he quickly changed the topic, she wondered if he might be...interested in her?

That seemed silly, though. She reasoned he was likely relieved that there wasn't another person he had to deal with for the hotel. It was just her and Ken, which was bad enough.

Not long after that question, Claire peeked at her watch and saw that it was fifteen after ten. A jolt of shock hit her and she stood up from her seat.

"Oh my gosh," she said. "I have to get home."

"Are you staying at the hotel tonight?" Chip asked. "There must be rooms you haven't gotten to yet."

Claire nodded, gathering her things. "Yes. I'm on the first floor tonight. What time do you want to meet tomorrow? I think Ken is supposed to bring some plans."

Chip shrugged. "You're the boss. You tell me."

"I don't feel like the boss," she said, shaking her head. "But how about eight?"

"Sounds good to me."

She said her goodbyes and rushed back to the cabin, worried that it was late enough that Marty might already be asleep.

That quickly stopped being her main worry, however, when she got to the cabin to find a car parked in the driveway. Her stomach dropped and her breathing froze. She had to force herself to keep driving.

She crept up the driveway slowly and when her headlights swung onto the car, her panic faded as she recognized it. It was Lucy's car.

Claire opened the cabin door to find a bit of a scene – Lucy was sitting on the couch, arms crossed, staring at Marty.

"Lucy!" she said, throwing her purse down. "I didn't know you were coming to visit!"

"And I didn't know you had company," Lucy said, eyebrows raised. "I thought this guy might've broken into your cabin."

Claire laughed. "Oh, well, not exactly. Haven't you met?"

Lucy stood up, shaking her head and giving Claire a hug. "No, we haven't. I got here twenty minutes ago and he wouldn't tell me who he was."

"Well," Marty said, "that's because I sort of did break into the cabin and I wasn't sure who *you* were."

Lucy's eyes darted between them. "Is this a prank or something?"

Oh dear. Claire had her work cut out for her. "Lucy, honey, why don't you take a seat?"

"What? Why?"

"Because what I'm going to tell you is quite shocking."

"Oh no." Lucy lowered herself onto the couch, never breaking eye contact. "Is he your boyfriend?"

Claire's mouth popped open in shock and Marty laughed.

"No," Claire said quickly. "Of course not."

Lucy giggled. "Sorry. I was just kidding."

Claire took a seat on the chair next to the couch. "Do you remember the DNA test that you girls got me for Christmas?"

She nodded slowly. "Yes?"

"Well, because of that test, I found your cousin. Meet Marty."

Claire watched Lucy's face go through the stages of understanding – first confusion, then excitement, and finally a scowl. "A cousin? How is that possible?"

Claire stood. "Let me make some tea. This will take some explaining."

She put the kettle on and started to tell the story to Lucy, who stopped her no less than a dozen times to interject her comments and questions.

Marty was quiet, mostly, laughing occasionally and watching them both.

Leaving out the bits about the FBI, Claire finished the story and showed Lucy the picture of baby Marty and Becca.

Lucy offered her opinion, as always, quite quickly. "This is insane."

"I know," said Claire.

Lucy shook her head. "At the same time, this might be the coolest thing that's ever happened to us."

Marty smiled. "Really?"

"Oh yeah." Lucy nodded enthusiastically, scooting closer to him. "You look just like her."

He shifted in his seat. "You mean my mom?"

Lucy shook her head. "Oh, I guess so. But I meant Claire."

"That makes sense," he said with a laugh.

Lucy put her hands up. "This is crazy! You got a match on the website and you didn't even tell us?"

Claire shook her head. "That's not exactly how it happened."

Marty cleared his throat. "You can tell her, Claire. Or I can."

Claire stared at him, frowning. "Are you sure?"

"Tell me what?" Lucy sat back, crossing her arms. "There's more? Do you have siblings?"

Marty shook his head. "No. I mean, not that I know of."

"Then what?" asked Lucy.

Claire bit her lip. It wasn't her secret to tell, so she just sat there, smiling at them both and admitting nothing.

Fortunately, Marty seemed to have made up his mind. "I'm not a computer hacker or anything, but I kind of went into the DNA system to get your mom's – I mean, Claire's – information."

Lucy cocked her head to the side. "Why? Doesn't the website give that to you?"

"Well..." He set his tea down. "It's complicated."

Lucy's eyes darted between them. "Complicated how?"

"Complicated like..." Marty let out a sigh. "Like I didn't know that I was adopted until a few weeks ago."

"Oh." Lucy's eyes grew wide.

"And," Marty continued, "I've been on the run for a few weeks, too."

Lucy stared at him for a beat, as though waiting for him to laugh. When he didn't, she asked, "On the run from who?"

Marty looked at Claire, then back at Lucy. "The FBI."

"Do you have warrants out?" Lucy dropped her voice. "Because I know a guy."

Claire blinked at her. "You *know* a guy?"

"Yeah!" Lucy said. "Margie's brother, what's-his-name."

Claire shook her head. "That's your guy?"

"I mean, I know other people, too," Lucy said, waving a hand.

Marty laughed, and Claire was relieved to see that Lucy had broken the tension.

"What'd you do?" Lucy asked, leaning forward.

Claire was slightly disturbed by how casually Lucy discussed breaking the law, but she reminded herself that Lucy was casual with most things.

"Nothing." Marty stopped and looked at Claire. "Is there a chance that the FBI might've gotten to Lucy already?"

Claire looked at her daughter. "I doubt it."

"Gotten to me?" Lucy repeated. "Like you think I'm wearing a wire?"

Claire laughed. The two of them were just too much. "Lucy, is there anything you're not telling us about your surprise visit?"

She put her hands up, the picture of innocence. "No! I just wanted to pop in and see how you were doing, and see this mysterious hotel you're working in."

She could tell that Lucy was trying to hide something. Her tone was off.

Claire narrowed her eyes at her. "Oh really? That's all?"

"Fine." Lucy let out a sigh. "I also thought they were going to fire me, so before they could do it, I quit my job."

Claire laughed. "Ah, that makes sense."

"The job didn't align with my professional interests anyway," Lucy continued. "That's all though, I swear. I don't know anything about the FBI."

Marty was smiling at her, but said nothing.

Lucy sighed again. "Really, that's it. Claire's been so busy working at this hotel that I wanted to make sure she was okay. And, you know, figure out my next steps, too."

Claire wasn't sure how many shocks Lucy could handle in one night, but she felt uncomfortable that Lucy still thought she was simply "working" at the hotel.

She'd hoped to tell the girls the truth about the hotel, and about the inheritance, the next time they all visited. It seemed she needed to move that date up, though.

Her silence didn't go unnoticed by Lucy. "What? Did you get fired, too?"

Claire shook her head. "No, I did not."

"They must not be paying you very well if you're staying in a place like this," Lucy said, shaking her head. "I mean, it's cute, but it's so small. How are we supposed to visit you here?"

Claire shrugged. "I was thinking you'd stay at the hotel."

"That'd be way too expensive."

Marty let out a laugh and Lucy shot him a look.

"What?" she said. "I'm a little bit broke, but I can always find ways to make money when I need to."

"That's not why I'm laughing," Marty said.

Lucy crossed her arms. "Then what is it?"

Claire let out a sigh. Whether the timing was right or not, Lucy needed to know the truth. "Do you think you can take another surprise?" she asked.

"Uh, I think so." Lucy shrugged. "Honestly, I thought the DNA test was going to be a super lame gift. It was Lillian's idea. This is actually pretty cool. Marty seems cool, except for the whole outlaw thing. But it kind of works for him."

Marty tilted his head. "It does?"

"Yeah."

Marty seemed pleased with that, though he was shaking his head.

"Does the hotel have a staff dorm?" asked Lucy. "Or servant quarters? Is it like Downton Abbey?"

"You could say it's kind of like Downton Abbey," Marty said.

Lucy narrowed her eyes. "I feel like I'm not in on the joke here, and I don't like it."

Claire knew that she needed to tell her the story of Uncle Robert's inheritance, but she was so tired, it felt like she was melting into the chair. "No, honey, it's not a joke."

"What do you mean?"

"I've been trying to find a good way to tell you this," Claire said slowly. "I'm not sure that there is a good way."

"That's okay. Just blurt it out," Lucy said.

Marty leaned forward. "I'll tell her."

That was one way to do it. Claire nodded. "Okay. Go for it."

Marty retold the story of Claire's inheritance the best that he could. He forgot Uncle Robert's name, but Lucy got the gist of the story.

By the end, Lucy had her jaw hanging open again. "How much money are we talking, Claire?"

"A lot," Claire said with a wince.

Lucy nodded. "Hm. I mean, I thought it was pretty crazy when you offered to pay off my student loans. I thought that was why I was getting some weird text messages from Bertie."

"Who's Bertie?" asked Marty.

"She's my cousin – one of Uncle Robert's kids. She was pretty salty, and now I get why."

Claire hadn't known about that. "I'm not working at the hotel, Lucy. I bought it."

Her eyes widened. "You *bought* it? Why?"

Claire covered her mouth, unsuccessfully fighting a yawn. "I don't know. I got laid off from work and it seemed silly to go back and try to find another job as a paralegal. Uncle Robert didn't want me to tell you girls about the money, and I didn't know what to do."

"So you bought a hotel? Here?"

"Yes." Claire nodded. "Well, I have a mortgage. I couldn't afford it outright. I thought it would be nice to be close to Margie, and she has that barn – you know, where she has weddings?"

Lucy nodded. "Yeah."

"Margie loves it here so much, and I wanted to build something on my own." Claire paused. "Uncle Robert told me that I should build the life I've always wanted."

Lucy pinched her lips together. "Aw! That's so sweet! I'm so happy for you. I really am."

Lucy jumped up to squeeze her into another hug.

Claire spoke again. "Do you want to see the hotel tonight? I'm heading over. They actually got a room ready for me."

Lucy shook her head. "No way. I need to talk to the man of mystery here. Can't you stay for the night?"

"I wish I could, but I don't want to upset the housekeeping staff. They already prepared the room."

Lucy put an arm around Claire. "Well, you should go then. You look exhausted. I can come over in the morning and check things out."

Claire let out another yawn. "That'd be nice."

"It's exciting to have a cousin that doesn't hate me," Lucy said, shooting a look at Marty.

"A cousin that doesn't hate you *yet*," Marty said with a smirk.

The room erupted into laughter. As much as Claire didn't want to leave them, it'd be bad for Marty if someone showed up at the cabin looking for her. It was best if she went back to the hotel and acted normally.

Claire settled on giving them each a hug goodbye. "Have fun."

Lucy nodded. "Sure. I'll be over in the morning."

Claire locked the door behind her, but before she went to her car, she paused to peek through the front window of the cabin. She could hear the rumbles of their laughter, and Lucy appeared to be rummaging through the cupboards, satisfied only when she found a box of microwave popcorn.

Claire smiled to herself. If only she could tell Uncle Robert – her life was already better than anything she could dream.

Chapter Fifteen

To think that Marty had initially been afraid of Lucy. When she'd first knocked on the door, he'd panicked and tried to hide.

Lucy had spotted him and rapped on the window, yelling, "I see you in there!"

She'd looked vaguely familiar from the photo albums, but at the time, he couldn't be certain she wasn't working with the FBI.

At least not until Claire returned after her night out with Chip. Then it became clear that Lucy was who she said she was, and that she was incapable of hiding anything.

Lucy returned to the couch with a bowl of popcorn and began a rapid-fire interrogation. He told her all about his unceremonious exit from working on SureFired, as well as his evasion of the FBI.

He felt awkward talking so much – he normally wasn't much of a talker – and decided to change the subject by asking her to tell him about her life.

"Okay," she said, smiling broadly. "It all started when I was born." She paused, then burst out laughing. "I'm just kidding. I won't go back that far. I mean, you already know about the plane crash. That's actually the first thing I remember."

"Really? You remember the crash?"

Lucy shook her head. "Not the crash itself. But I remember being afraid of planes, even when they flew overhead. It used to freak me out. Claire had to take me to a kid therapist."

"Oh yeah?" Maybe if Marty's parents had taken him to a therapist, they could've found a way to tell him he was adopted.

"I still can't get on a plane." Lucy let out a sigh. "Claire took all of us to therapy, but I was the oldest and actually, you know, knew that my parents were gone."

"How old were your sisters? When the accident happened."

"They weren't even one yet," Lucy said. "To them, Claire's always been Mom. But to me, I had a mom, and Aunt Claire was always Aunt Claire."

He frowned. "I'm sorry."

"It's okay. She's great. And I should be over it by now." Lucy stared into space for a moment before snapping her attention back to him. "What about you? You said you'd just found out you were adopted?"

He nodded. "Yeah, a few weeks ago. For those few weeks, I thought my biological mom was alive. Now I find out she's gone so...yeah."

Lucy covered her mouth with her hand. "Oh my gosh, I'm sorry. You lost your mom in the plane crash too."

"What did people say about her? What was she like?" asked Marty.

Lucy sat back, squinting her eyes, deep in thought. "I don't know. When I was younger, no one really talked about her – except for Claire. She'd talk about everyone who'd died in the crash, tell us their favorite movies and foods. She tried to keep us connected, you know?"

Marty nodded. "That's nice."

"Then when I got older, things started slipping out," Lucy said. "From other people, I mean. They'd say that your mom was fun, and wild, and that she had an addiction problem."

"Ah." Marty nodded. "When she was living with my parents – my adoptive parents – I think she was healthy. They said she just seemed sad."

"Really?" Lucy pondered this for a moment. "Maybe she should've stayed with them and not gone to that rehab. Things might've all turned out differently."

Marty hadn't thought of that. "Maybe."

"When were you born?"

He cleared his throat. "November 7th, 1992."

"Right, so just a few months before the crash." Lucy waved a hand. "I'm sorry, I don't mean to say stuff like that. It just pops in my head – other possible lives. You know?"

He smiled. "Yeah."

"That was dumb, I'm sorry," Lucy said. "I'm pretty sure Aunt Becca called Grandma and asked for help, actually. Becca said she'd been doing great, but it all fell apart and she didn't know where to go."

He frowned. He felt sorry for his mother. Giving him up must've been hard on her. Or at least, that's what he'd like to believe – that he wasn't easy to leave behind.

Lucy proceeded to tell him about the rest of her life. She and her sisters went to public school, and true to what Claire had said, it didn't seem like they'd ever had much money.

Lucy got into college "by the skin of her teeth," as she put it, and was open about her struggles.

"I changed majors three times, usually after I failed one of the core classes. After a while, an advisor sat me down and told me that if I couldn't figure out what I wanted, then I should stop wasting everyone's time."

Marty pulled back. "Whoa. That's not nice or helpful."

Lucy shrugged. "It worked. I left college after that. He'd told me there was no hope of recovering my GPA, and that my degree wouldn't be worth anything."

"That's just not true," Marty said, shaking his head. He, too, had wished he'd finished his degree, but no one had sabotaged him but himself. "That advisor lied to you."

"Yeah, well, I was young and easily discouraged. Tale as old as time." She picked out a half-popped kernel from the bottom of the bowl and crushed it in her teeth. "It doesn't matter. Even if I went back today, I don't know what I'd go for."

"Too many possible lives?"

She pointed a finger at him. "Exactly. Why would I want to limit myself like that?"

There was no longer any doubt in Marty's mind about Lucy not working with the FBI. She spoke freely and without pretense, which was quite different from Claire, who had a sort of quiet reserve. There was nothing quiet or reserved about Lucy, and while Marty usually found people like that to be off-putting, he didn't feel that way now.

He wasn't sure why. He should be more suspicious, since he was in a vulnerable position, seemingly without a friend in the world. Except Claire, of course.

Claire's words kept echoing in his mind. "We're still family."

"I can't believe your job," Lucy said, ripping him out of his thoughts.

"Oh, you mean the CEO?"

She nodded. "Him, and what he did to you. As much as I didn't like my old boss, at least he didn't try to frame me for espionage."

Marty laughed. "Yeah, that was a new one for me too."

"You said someone warned you? That the police were waiting at your car?"

"Oh. That was one of my old coworkers, David Marilyn."

"David Marilyn," Lucy repeated. "Could you get evidence that you're innocent if he could get you back in the system?"

He thought on this for a moment. "Probably."

"Maybe he'll help you, then."

"I don't think so, and I'm too afraid to ask." Marty said with a frown.

"Why? Who cares?"

Marty laughed. "Dave wouldn't want to help. Even if someone did, I'm considered a spy now, so it's too dangerous for them to even talk to me."

Really, if anyone knew how bad things were with Sure-Fired, it was the CEO's secretary. She had been in the meeting where Marty first spoke up, and she had surely seen all of the emails and memos showing that testing had failed.

But she was a single mom with two kids. She couldn't speak up even if she wanted to. The CEO had threatened to fire her over minor inconveniences, and had her in a broad non-compete agreement. Sure, the agreement saying she couldn't work basically anywhere in a hundred-mile radius wouldn't hold up in court, but Marty knew she couldn't afford an attorney. The CEO knew that too. He wouldn't show her any mercy if she talked.

Marty wouldn't put that on her, or on anyone.

Lucy frowned. "That's unfortunate for your situation, then."

"I'm pretty sure that if I even approached Dave, a bunch of helicopters would drop out of the sky and come after me."

Lucy laughed. "I can see it now. It'd be one of those fire-fighting helicopters. You know the ones. They scoop up water in those big buckets and dump it on the flames."

"Yeah," he said with a smile. "They'd drop me off in a forest somewhere and you'd never see me again."

She sighed. "That'd be a shame. You're the only cousin who doesn't hate me. Unless you just started hating me."

He laughed. "No. I don't hate you."

"Good." Lucy smiled. "I was thinking, what if I talked to David for you?"

That was a nice thought, but he didn't want anyone else to get involved. "You'd probably end up getting arrested too."

Lucy rolled her eyes. "That's stupid. Do you have any friends who are attorneys?"

He shook his head. "Unfortunately no, but Claire has someone in mind. They can't meet with us – with her – for a few weeks though."

"That stinks. I'm sorry. I'm sure this is a sore subject."

He shook his head. "No, it's been really nice to talk. I've been sitting here alone every day, just brooding."

She nodded knowingly. "You do seem like the brooding type."

"Hey!"

Lucy laughed. "Don't worry, Marty. I'm sure we can figure it out." She yawned and stretched. "I'm sorry, but I'm actually pretty tired. And if I need to check out this hotel that Claire apparently owns in the morning, I should get to bed."

"Sure. It's getting late."

"Goodnight, cousin who doesn't hate me!" she called out as she walked into the next room.

Marty set himself up on the couch and tried to quiet his thoughts. He couldn't get over the fact that Lucy offered to help him. She barely knew him.

Was this what having a big family was like? He'd never had much family growing up. He didn't have siblings and wasn't close with his cousins.

If so, it was nice. Maybe Uncle Robert had gotten it right in giving all that money to Claire. She had a nice family. Marty felt lucky to be connected to them.

He closed his eyes and drifted off.

Chapter Sixteen

The room Claire slept in that night was close to the elevators, and though noise from comings and goings made its way in, she was so tired that she barely noticed. She slept heavily, dead to the world, and didn't open her eyes until her alarm went off the next morning.

It took her a moment to regain her senses, and memories from the night before came flooding in. There was a lot to unpack. She was excited that Lucy was visiting, and touched by how well Lucy and Marty got along.

Her feelings were less clear about her evening with Chip. It was lovely. He was so interesting and...passionate. It seemed like they were finally getting along, too, which was nice.

He wouldn't appreciate it if she were late for their morning meeting, though, so she leapt out of bed and hurried to the shower.

The water pressure was good, but the shower itself suffered from the same issues as the others in the hotel. The fixtures were a bit loose, and the grout around the tiles was cracking and flaking. Antique charm was something she appreciated, but no one appreciated crumbling grout.

She added "shower updates" to her notebook and quickly dried her hair.

Once she was ready, she sent a text message to check when Lucy planned to stop by.

She responded quickly. "I'm a little slow this morning. Maybe in an hour or so?"

"No problem. Anytime is good for me," she wrote back before dabbing on a touch of makeup and packing up her bag.

She was about to leave when the room phone rang.

"Hello?" she said, picking up the receiver. It was a heavy, antique-style phone, with brushed silver and gold on the rotary plate. It stood on four opulent feet, the base decorated in weaving designs.

Claire loved it. True, the rotary spinner was less useful than a push-button phone, but it was so charming. It made her feel like she'd stepped back in time.

"You've got a visitor," said a bored voice. "Should I send her up?"

"I'm just leaving my room now, Gigi. Do you know who the visitor is?"

Silence for a moment. "I think she said her name is Barbie."

Hm. "Tell her I'll be right there."

Claire swung her bag onto her shoulder and walked down the hall to the lobby. Margie was standing at the front desk, trying to make conversation with Gigi.

"Morning!" Claire called out before flopping her bag onto the counter. "Gigi, can you please hold this for me?"

Gigi nodded and extended a hand to grab the bag, tucking it under the desk.

Claire turned to Margie and smiled. "It's nice to see you today. I actually had another visitor yesterday."

Margie's eyes grew wide. "You mean they came back?"

Claire looked around. "What? Who?"

"Claire," Margie said loudly. "I love the Madrona trees out in the front. Can we go look at them?"

Claire had no idea what had gotten into Margie, but she agreed. "Sure."

They walked through the front doors and into the brisk air. The sky was a gorgeous, bright blue, a shining contrast to the hotel's sandy colored stone.

Margie kept walking until they reached one of the two large Madrona trees in front of the hotel. It towered over them, its red bark peeling in sheets that crunched beneath their feet.

Margie spoke in a lower voice. "Hank told me something concerning last night."

"What was it?"

Margie clenched her hands together, looking around before answering. "He said that he'd gotten a report about the FBI's most wanted list."

"And?"

"Marty is on the list," she said in a whisper.

Claire leaned in. "How is that possible?"

"I don't know!" Margie said. "He told me they'd had some excitement and that one of the FBI's most wanted may be on the islands. I woke up and took the first ferry to tell you. I just had to see you!"

Claire pulled out her cell phone. "Is the list public?"

"I think so," Margie said, leaning over Claire's shoulder.

Claire typed in "FBI's Most Wanted List" and quickly found what she was looking for. She frowned as she scrolled through the names and faces. "These guys look scary."

"I know!" Margie said. She stuck a finger and stopped on a picture. "Look at that one!"

Margie's finger accidentally opened the man's poster. She gasped. "It says he's wanted for *murder!* Are they all murderers?"

Claire cleared her throat. "Of course not. Marty isn't a murderer."

Margie shot her a concerned look, but said nothing.

"This is the top ten most wanted," Claire continued, clicking back to the main list. "I doubt that he's on the top ten people they –"

Just then, she saw him. Her mouth popped open. "There he is."

"Is that him?" Margie asked. "But he's so cute! He doesn't look like a murderer at all."

"It's an old picture, but that's him," Claire said, clicking on it.

Margie read it aloud. "Marty Coursin, date of birth used: November 7th, 1992."

Claire stared at it for a moment. "November."

"Was that before the accident, Claire?"

She nodded, hurriedly scrolling down, past the pictures of Marty with a computer-generated beard, then another with fake-looking long hair. She read the next section. "The FBI is offering a reward of up to $200,000 for information directly leading to the arrest of Marty Coursin."

"Oh my..." Margie said.

Claire read on. "Caution: Marty Coursin is wanted for espionage. He has connections to Seattle, the San Juan Islands, Spain, and China. Coursin speaks fluent Spanish."

"Oh, he speaks Spanish!" Margie said, delighted.

Claire almost laughed. This was ridiculous. "What an odd thing to include."

"Well," Margie said, dropping her voice again, "they might've added that because he could flee to Spain."

Claire let out a sigh and put the phone back into her purse. "He's not going to flee to Spain."

"How do you know?"

Claire looked over her shoulder before responding, voice hushed. "Because he's staying with me!"

Margie let out a gasp. "Claire, it said he's a spy. And he should be considered armed and extremely dangerous!"

Claire shook her head. "It's not true. He's been framed. He's just a kid, after all."

"A thirty-year old kid."

"Twenty-nine," Claire corrected.

Margie studied her silently, eyes wide and lips pursed. The only thing they could hear was a loud boat buzzing by on the water.

Claire let out a sigh. "He's innocent, Margie. He's not a spy. He's a kid who got mixed up with the wrong company."

Margie rung her hands together. "Are you sure you don't want me to tell Hank?"

"No." Claire looked around, trying to think of how to convince Margie not to panic. "He's a sweet kid. He's just like Becca, and reminds me so much of her. Lucy dropped by last night. I didn't expect her, so I was surprised, but the two of them became the fastest of friends."

Margie smiled and was about to say something when she was interrupted by a deep, bellowing voice.

"Good morning, ladies!"

Claire turned around. It was Chip, waving at them from the parking lot.

Margie dropped her voice low again. "Who's that?"

"The general manager of the hotel."

"The one who doesn't like you?" asked Margie.

Claire elbowed her subtly in the ribs. "Hey, Chip!" she called out.

"Because he's smiling at you like he likes you," Margie said as she waved.

Claire wanted to elbow her again, but Chip had already reached them.

"Beautiful day, isn't it?" he said.

"It is," Claire said, forcing a smile. "Am I late for our meeting?"

"No, of course not. You're never late." He smiled and nodded at Margie. "Hi. Nice to meet you. I'm Chip."

Margie extended a hand to shake. "Hi Chip! I'm Claire's friend Margie."

"I've heard so much about you," he said. "Did you come by for a tour?"

Claire shot Margie a look, which Margie expertly avoided. "You know, I would *love* a tour."

"Come on in."

He started walking ahead of them, and Margie followed. "I live on San Juan Island. Do you know Hank Kowalski? He's the Chief Deputy Sheriff."

Chip turned around and smiled. "Oh yeah, of course I know Hank. Great guy."

Margie smiled, and Claire knew what was coming. She was powerless to stop it, just as Margie was powerless to stop herself from trying to set Claire up with every guy they ever knew. She'd tried to force many romances over the years – the girls' soccer coach, a substitute teacher, even Margie's brother Mike.

"Hank is my husband," Margie said brightly.

Chip nodded. "No kidding."

Margie continued. "Claire is single though, as you probably know."

Claire closed her eyes. This was going to be a long tour.

Chapter Seventeen

T his friend of Claire's was a hoot. Chip could hardly keep up with her. When she wasn't asking questions, she was filling the silence with stories from the past, mostly about Claire.

It took them half an hour just to walk through the lobby. Chip was having a great time, but he thought Claire seemed tense.

When Margie got distracted by a conversation with two passing guests, Chip stepped aside with Claire. "Is everything okay?"

Claire smiled. "Yes, of course. Why?"

"You seem..." Chip shrugged. "Not yourself. We don't have to continue the tour. I'm sure you're busy."

"No, it's not that." Claire's eyes lingered on him, searching.

Searching for what? Words? Studying him? He didn't know. Chip lost his breath for a moment. Claire had been on his mind constantly since their outing the night before. He felt positively bewitched by her.

At that moment, he had two simultaneous thoughts: how lucky he was to have her attention again, and what a mess it would be to fall in love with his boss.

He cleared his throat. "Please, tell me. I'm here to help."

A smile flashed on her face, then quickly faded. "It's –"

"They're loving their stay!" Margie said triumphantly, rejoining the conversation.

"Er – who is?" Claire asked.

"That couple I just talked to," said Margie. "They just got married a few months ago and decided to make the trip as a little getaway. So sweet!"

Chip smiled. "That's nice to hear."

"Where were we?" asked Margie, beaming.

At Margie's prompting, Chip pointed out a few aspects of the lobby and explained the challenges of maintaining the Art Deco appearance. Margie was nodding enthusiastically and Chip suddenly realized he might be making a fool of himself.

"I'm sorry," he said to Margie. "You've already heard about the hotel, haven't you?"

She smiled and waved a hand. "Just a bit, and it was always quite brief." Margie looked around, admiring the chandelier above them. "Steve was a friend of mine, but we usually met over in Friday Harbor. How's he doing?"

"He's good. I just talked to him a few weeks ago." Chip felt a pang of shame. The last time he'd spoken to Steve, he was still angry about Claire, still convinced that she would be the bane of his existence. How wrong he'd been.

Margie walked toward one of the windows overlooking the water. "The first time that Hank brought me to Orcas Island, Steve accused me of stealing from him."

Chip cocked his head to the side. "Stealing?"

"Well, he called that little bay out there Sunset Cove, because of the beautiful sunsets you can catch behind the mountain. And I thought that was just wonderful, and I told him that my wedding venue was named Saltwater Cove."

"Ah." Chip smiled. "I can see where this is going."

"Mhm," Margie said with a nod. "Steve said that he couldn't believe I had the audacity to come to *his* hotel and steal one of *his* names. I was mortified, and I apologized several times, at one point promising to change the name of my business and everything."

Chip laughed. "Then Steve told you that he was joking."

"Yes!" Margie said, shaking her head. "He did. He laughed so hard that he cried. Hank laughed at me too! They were terrible. On the way home I saw that every other road on this island had Cove in the name."

"That's Steve for you," Chip said, shaking his head.

"I'm sure you miss him." Margie patted him on the shoulder.

"Of course," he said, "but –"

Margie cut in. "But Claire is a *great* new Steve, isn't she?"

He nodded, and before he could form a response, Margie spoke again. "I'm sure she makes the loveliest boss, but she's so much more than that. She's kind and beautiful, too."

Chip looked at Claire, who was staring down at the ground, and he couldn't help himself. "Yes, she most certainly is."

"Okay Margie," Claire said loudly. "Is there anything else you wanted to see today?"

"If any of the rooms are open, I'd love to take a peek."

From the narrowing of Claire's eyes, it didn't seem like this was the response she was looking for.

Chip, however, was having a grand time and was happy to extend the tour. He cleared his throat. "No problem. Let me check our system and grab some room keys."

He popped over to the front desk, momentarily excusing Gigi from her post. As he clicked around the computer, Chip was disappointed to see that there were more than a few rooms open. He did a quick count. The hotel had twenty-one unoccupied rooms.

While it was nice to have something to show Margie, it was another sad reminder of how empty they were running. He hoped that there were better days ahead of them.

There was hope, of course. Claire had shocked him the previous night with the story of that inheritance. True, she didn't have experience in hotels, but that didn't matter. She was willing to learn.

What was more important was that she wasn't counting on the hotel to make her a fortune. She already had a fortune, and she wanted the hotel for the right reasons.

Or so it seemed.

Chip returned with the keys to find that Claire had another visitor – a young woman with striking red hair.

He said hello and Claire introduced them. "I'd like you to meet my eldest daughter, Lucy."

Chip shook her hand. "I've heard so much about you. It's nice to meet you."

"All good things, I hope?" Lucy asked.

"Of course," Chip said.

Lucy let out a breath, puffing out her cheeks. "Then Claire has been lying."

He and Margie laughed while Claire maintained a tight smile.

"Is everything okay, sweetie?" asked Claire.

Lucy shrugged. "Yeah. I just wanted to stop by and check this place out."

"We were just about to go and see some rooms," Margie said. "Maybe Claire can tell us about some of the improvements she has in mind."

Lucy's eyes brightened. "I had some ideas for improvements, too."

Margie clapped her hands together excitedly. "Do tell!"

"Well, first of all," Lucy said, "the website looks like it fell out of the nineties."

Claire stepped forward. "I thought it looked nice."

"I'm no computer wizard," Lucy continued, "but I think even I could make something better."

Chip crossed his arms. "Go on."

"It's not just the website, it's the pictures, too." Lucy took a breath. "I used to work at this design studio. I'm not a designer, but I was an administrative assistant to the director – and I'd always hear him say that we needed to make things beautiful so people could envision themselves there."

"Oh. I like that," said Margie.

"I don't get that from the website," Lucy said. "The pictures of the rooms, even of this lobby, do nothing for me. Now that I'm here, though, I'm like 'Wow! This place is unbelievable!'"

A smile – a real smile – crossed Claire's face. "You like it, then?"

"Yes! It's gorgeous!" Lucy stopped and looked at Chip. "I'm sorry. Are you the website guy?"

He was not, but Chip wasn't going to let that stop him from having some fun. "Yes. I am the website guy. I do all of the websites. That's my job here."

Lucy visibly cringed. "I didn't mean to be rude. It just needs a little, uh, you know, pick-me-up. Maybe I could help?"

"I know someone who can take the pictures," Margie offered.

Chip shook his head. "No, it's too late. She's right. I'm terrible at this job. I've been looking for a sign that I should leave, and I think this is it."

Lucy's mouth dropped open. "You're not terrible! I'm sure you can fix it!"

Chip stared at her for a moment, but he was unable to keep himself from laughing. Claire and Margie joined in as Lucy stood there, dumbfounded.

"He's teasing you, Lucy," Claire said.

Chip shrugged. "It was too easy."

"Oh phew." Lucy put a hand to her chest. "I really get myself in trouble sometimes."

"The website was set up by the old owner's nephew," Chip continued. "I agree. It needs some work."

"Something to add to the list," Claire said with a smile. "Shall we finish this tour, then?"

Chip nodded and led them down the hallway. He had keys for rooms on the first, second, and third floors, so they started from the bottom and made their way up.

Margie had a ton of questions, and Chip was happy to answer them. It also gave Claire an opportunity to show him some of the things she'd noticed in the rooms. He was ashamed to admit that he hadn't paid much attention to the aging power outlets or to the crumbling grout in the bathrooms.

"I am a bit worried about how much everything will cost, though," said Claire, biting her lip.

"You'll figure it out," Margie said. "Don't worry."

Claire didn't respond, and Margie moved to gushing about the antique telephone at the bedside.

"Would you look at that!" she said, lifting the receiver and holding it to her ear. "This is adorable. Claire, you have to tell me where I can get one of these for my house."

Claire smiled. "I'd be happy to, but I think they're as old the hotel itself."

"No!" Margie pulled the receiver away from her face, marveling at it.

Chip nodded. "Yeah, we found those in an old storage room a few years ago and decided to refurbish and install them. They're not as fancy as new phones, but people seem to love them."

"Do you like them, Claire?" asked Lucy, eyeing the phone suspiciously.

Claire didn't answer at first. It seemed like she'd zoned out.

Lucy waved her arms. "Earth to Claire."

"Oh yes," she said, smiling. "I like them very much."

"All right." Lucy frowned. "Then I guess I'm outnumbered."

"What's not to like?" asked Margie. "They're charming."

"Hm." Lucy stood back, looking around the room. "I guess that's kind of what you're going for here, isn't it?"

Claire laughed. "Yeah, it kind of is."

"Then you've done a great job," Lucy said with a smile.

They toured the second and third rooms, and once they were done, Margie announced that she was taking Lucy to breakfast at the Plum Spoon.

"That way you two can catch up on business things," she said, pulling Lucy by the arm. "We'll see you later, Claire."

Claire seemed to not hear her at first. After a beat, she nodded and waved them off.

"Goodbye!" Margie called out.

Chip turned to her and cleared his throat. "Would now be a good time to go over the budget for improvements, or are you meeting with Ken?"

"Ah, no. I don't know where Ken is."

He stared at her, for perhaps a moment too long. He needed to cool it.

Chip smiled, making sure not to stare this time. "Shall we?"

Claire nodded. "Sure."

Chapter Eighteen

They took the stairs down to Chip's office. Claire was glad to have a moment to gather her thoughts as Chip fired up his computer.

Though finding out that Marty was now on the FBI's Most Wanted List was an unpleasant surprise, she'd made up her mind that it didn't change things. The FBI had already been looking for him. What difference did a list make? Would a measly two-hundred-thousand-dollar reward really prompt people to turn him in?

She was lost in thought when she heard Chip say, "If we can budget four hundred thousand for the bathrooms – "

"I'm sorry," she said, interrupting him. "Did you say four hundred *thousand?*"

He looked down at the paper on his desk, then back up at her. "Yeah, I think that sounds about right. That's if we fully renovate the bathrooms, of course. Each one will run about ten thousand, and we've got almost forty of them."

Claire took a sip of water. A few months ago, she'd refused to try the new restaurant in her neighborhood because she thought charging twenty-one dollars for a burrito was a crime.

"That's a lot of money," she finally said.

"We don't have to fully renovate them," he continued. "I can get estimates for redoing the tile, and maybe replacing the tubs?"

Claire nodded. "Yes. I'd like to see how that compares."

She wasn't even sure how much money she still had in the bank. Could she get a loan for improvements?

Chip clicked away, typing on his keyboard. "All right, I've added that. I wanted to get some estimates to revamp the landscaping, too. I think Lucy might be right about our curb appeal."

"Right," Claire said with a nod. "Landscaping."

Her phone dinged, and she pulled it out of her purse to see a message from Margie. "Is Chip single? Asking for a friend."

She frowned and slipped her phone back into her purse. From now on, Margie wasn't allowed to talk to Chip. Claire needed him to take her seriously, and it seemed like their working relationship was finally taking a turn for the better.

Claire didn't want to ruin it by making him think she was hitting on him. She was the boss! That would be harassment. The poor man had the right to do his job in peace, even if he was rapidly becoming a silver fox.

Claire felt a flash of embarrassment for even thinking the phrase "silver fox." It was Margie's fault.

"Are you okay?" Chip asked.

She looked up, forcing a smile. "Yes, why?"

"You just let out a big sigh."

Oh dear. "I did? Sorry. I just have a lot on my mind."

He sat back, resting his hands on the desk. "Listen, I know I can be challenging."

"You're not challenging."

He put up a hand. "Please, you don't have to humor me. I know I scare the staff. I don't intend to, but I also don't try not to."

Claire smiled. "Whatever you're doing, it's working."

"Except it isn't." He rubbed his face with one hand, then spoke again. "You've seen the numbers. We need a huge change to keep this hotel afloat. I don't want you to lose your investment."

"I'm sure we can figure it out."

He nodded. "I'm sure we can, too. I think we make a great team. I really do, and I'm sorry that I was so...myself when we first met."

That made Claire laugh. "I wasn't at my best, either."

"The truth is, I'm not proud of who I used to be, and sometimes I overdo it, trying to make up for my past."

"I'm not sure what you mean," she said.

Chip shifted in his chair, leaning forward. "You made a joke last night about me crashing the economy."

"That wasn't serious!" Claire needed to be careful about what she said to him.

He shook his head. "No, I know. But I'm not entirely innocent."

"Chip –"

He continued. "I worked at an investment bank. I'd been there for seventeen years, and I knew what they were doing."

Claire frowned. She never fully understood the economic crash. All she knew was the little pension she'd hoped to one day receive had been wiped out. She'd chalked it up to bad luck.

"I'm embarrassed to admit this," she said, "but I don't even know what caused the crash. Wasn't it people buying homes they couldn't afford?"

Sort of like what Claire was doing now, except it was a hotel and not a home. Her stomach sank at the thought.

"No, that wasn't it." Chip shifted again. It looked like he was in pain. "It was easy to put the blame on the average person, but that wasn't it at all. The banks – they knew what they were doing. They preyed on people. There were teams trained to do this, to find someone who was in the market for a house and sell them a mortgage they couldn't afford."

This still sounded a bit too much like what Claire had done with the hotel. "They shouldn't have gotten those homes, though, right?"

"It wasn't the home they couldn't afford. The banks sold them a mortgage with a low interest rate, and everything looked fine. They'd sign, they'd make their payments, and then in a year or two, the interest rate would climb and climb until they couldn't keep up."

Claire frowned. She thought she'd gotten a fixed rate for the hotel, but what if she hadn't? The room was starting to feel hot.

He was speaking quickly now. "They hid that from people. They didn't care that people would lose their homes. That was the point. They wanted to take as much money from them as they could, as fast as they could."

Claire shrugged. "That's what banks do, isn't it?"

"That's the thing. The banks weren't happy just ruining those lives. They then said, 'Hey look at these great mortgages we have, you can sink your retirement money into these, it's a great, safe investment.' They sold them off to pension funds and 401ks, even though they *knew* the home owners weren't going to be able to keep making payments. They knew it would all fall apart, and the pensions would lose everything, and the home owners would lose everything, and they did it anyway."

"Wow. I didn't know that." Claire sat for a moment. "That's...much worse than I realized."

"Exactly." He nodded. "I worked at that bank for seventeen years, and though I didn't work on one of those teams, I started to hear things. I started to see things."

Claire wanted to reach across the table and give him a hug. He looked tortured. "It's okay, Chip. It's not like you came up with it."

He flinched. "That's nice of you to say, but it's not okay. I could've looked into it. I could've figured out what was going on. I could've done something about it, even if it didn't stop it, I could've *tried*."

"Well, I'm sorry that you couldn't prevent the world financial crash of 2008," Claire said with a laugh. "Maybe next time?"

He laughed, too. "I know I might've made no difference. It's just the fact that..." He trailed off.

She waited for him to finish.

He spoke again. "It's the fact that I didn't care. I knew something was off, but I figured so what, we're all making money, that's what matters."

"Ah, I understand."

"It was all for nothing, too." Chip stared at her. "I lost my retirement. I lost my job. I lost my wife – not because of the crash, but because of how I was, for far too long, just interested in chasing the next dollar."

Claire smiled. "So now we need to spend four hundred thousand dollars on the bathrooms?"

He laughed, heartily. "No, of course not. I just don't make all of my decisions because of money anymore. When something is wrong, I speak up. Maybe too much. For that, I'm sorry."

It didn't seem like too much to Claire. It seemed like a lesson hard learned. She leaned forward and let out a breath. "Don't be sorry. I like working with you. I like that you're honest. I...like you. I trust you."

He smiled. "I trust you too."

At that moment, the fax machine behind Chip sprung to life. Claire watched as it noisily printed a sheet of paper with Marty's face prominently displayed at the top.

Chapter Nineteen

E ven with extremely heavy hinting, Lucy couldn't keep Margie from asking about Marty as they ate their meal in the hotel restaurant. She finally had to say, "How about we discuss this later, *outside*?"

The realization dawned on Margie, and she nodded, shooting a wink at Lucy. "Good idea."

They quickly finished their meals – Lucy was genuinely surprised that the hotel's food was so good – and exited through the patio.

"I am sorry about that," Margie said as they walked along the water. "I wasn't thinking. I'm not used to a life of crime."

Lucy let out a little laugh. "It's okay. It's hard to get into the mindset that you're being watched by the FBI."

They continued down the path and Lucy savored the solitude around them. She liked the sound of the crushed stone under her feet. She liked the calls of the seabirds that carried across the water. The ocean was peaceful, and the sun had just started reaching over the mountain, causing the water to sparkle.

"You probably haven't heard this yet," Margie said, stopping to look around. She dropped her voice. "Marty was added to the FBI's Top Ten Most Wanted list."

This didn't trouble Lucy as much as it should have. She shrugged. "It happens to the best of us."

Margie laughed. "I'm serious!"

"So am I," Lucy said.

"You're too much." Margie shook her head. "Tell me about him. What's he like?"

Lucy told Margie everything she knew so far, from Marty's secret adoption, to his legal troubles, to his impressive camping skills.

When she finished, Margie stopped and stared at her. Lucy felt uncomfortable with her silence.

"Well? What do you think?" asked Lucy.

Margie crossed her arms. "I don't know."

That wasn't the type of response she was hoping for.

Margie sighed and spoke again. "Don't you think it'd be better if he just turned himself in and explained all of this?"

"Maybe." After thinking for a moment, Lucy shook her head. "What good is an explanation, though, when he has no evidence to support it? It's his word against theirs, and they have 'proof.'"

Margie rung her hands together. "I suppose so."

Her phone went off, and she reached into her purse to retrieve it. "Oh no."

"What?" Lucy asked, leaning in.

"It's a text from Claire. She needs us to come and distract Chip in his office. She said he got a fax."

Lucy narrowed her eyes. "A fax? Is that code for something?"

"I don't know, but we'd better get going. We're a good ten-minute walk from the hotel."

They rushed back, cutting through the restaurant and past the front desk. It took a minute of searching, but they found the heavy wooden door marked "Manager." It had a frosted glass window and inside, they could make out the muffled voices of Chip and Claire.

"What should we do?" Lucy whispered.

Margie was already two steps ahead of her, turning the doorknob as she knocked. "Hello hello!" she called out, a broad smile spanning her face.

Lucy forced herself to smile and followed Margie inside.

"Oh, hi Margie," Claire said.

Lucy looked over to Chip, sitting at the large, stately desk at the back of the room. Squarely behind him she spotted the fax machine, which was sporting a black-and-white printout of Marty's face.

So fax wasn't a code word. Who even used fax machines anymore? Ridiculous.

"We just had the loveliest brunch, and I was hoping that you two might want to come and join us for a walk along the water?" Margie said, casually strolling over to Chip and putting a hand on his shoulder.

Chip turned and looked up at her. "I'm glad to hear that you enjoyed the Plum Spoon, but I'm going to have to skip the walk. Claire's putting me to work today. I'm getting bids for some hotel improvements."

"What a shame!" said Margie, giving Lucy a stern stare.

Lucy took the hint, and started slowly moving toward Chip's desk.

Margie kept talking. "I know a wonderful photographer who could take new pictures of the property, if you're interested?"

He looked at Claire, then back at Margie. "Sure. That'd be great."

How was Lucy going to get behind that huge desk without looking suspicious? She walked slowly, careful not to bump any of the leaning towers of papers on the surrounding bookshelves.

As she rounded a chair, Lucy's foot got caught on a rug and she went tumbling to the ground.

"Lucy!" said Claire, getting up from her seat. "Are you okay?"

"Oof." Lucy did her best impression of a professional soccer player, sprawled and immobile.

Chip stood up from his desk and rushed over. "I'm so sorry! It's an old rug and people hardly ever come in here. Are you all right?"

Lucy sat up slowly. She could see Margie silently inching toward the fax machine before snatching the paper and shoving it into her pocket.

"I'm fine, just a bit...surprised." She stood up, dusting herself off.

"You have to be careful," said Claire, genuinely concerned about Lucy's health.

"I'm sorry, I'm just clumsy," she said, patting Claire on the hand. "Will you be working all day?"

Claire nodded. "Yes, I think so. If you want to head back to the cabin, I could meet you there later?"

"Sure." Lucy nodded slowly. "I'll go back now?"

Claire shrugged. "Yeah, that sounds good."

Margie and Lucy said their goodbyes and made their exit. Chip seemed none the wiser, cheerfully waving them off and making them promise to return soon.

Once they were back in the parking lot, Lucy asked to see the printout.

"Why are they using ancient technology to torment us?" Lucy groaned.

"It's not ancient, it's useful. Especially if they don't have an email for the hotel." Margie paused. "Do you think they might've emailed it, too?"

"They must have, but maybe Claire can take care of that? I'll text her." Lucy pulled out her phone and sent a less-than-cryptic text to Claire that read, "Check your email, too. I bet the hotel gets lots of SPAM!"

"I unplugged the fax machine," Margie said. "There won't be any more surprises."

Lucy nodded, impressed. "Nice."

"Now what should we do?"

Lucy looked around. It still didn't seem like the FBI was descending upon them. At least not yet. They had some time.

"I think Claire wanted me to go back and check on Marty, so I'll do that."

Margie put her hands on her hips. "What should I do?"

"You need to put all of your effort into not telling anyone about this."

Margie frowned. "Fair point. It's only getting harder. I should be getting back anyway. I'm supposed to meet with a client later today."

"Okay, you go!" Lucy said, walking toward her car. "And excellent work in there."

Margie smiled. "You too."

Lucy would never admit that her fall wasn't intentional. She wasn't the best under pressure, but sometimes chaos worked in her favor.

When Lucy got back to the cabin, it looked abandoned. All of the lights were off and there was no sign of life.

"Hello?" she called out. It was actually quite creepy. "It's Lucy. Is anyone home?"

There was a rustling noise from the loft and Marty popped his head out. "Are they still here?" he asked in a hoarse voice.

"Is who still here?"

He let out a sigh, climbing down the ladder. "The FBI agents. A car pulled up outside of the house, and I thought it was you or Claire, but I saw them instead. They poked around outside and came up to the door."

Lucy tried not to react, but she couldn't help making a face. "That's not good."

"I know. I think I need to pack up and get back to camping," he said.

"That's not a long-term solution, Marty." Lucy paused. "Also, things have gotten a tad worse."

Marty raised an eyebrow. "What does that mean?"

She told him about the FBI's Most Wanted List, as well as the fact that the hotel received a fax with his information on it.

"They're going to be looking everywhere for you. I'm betting every ferry is being watched, too."

The color drained from his face. "I'm going to die in prison, aren't I?"

"No!" said Lucy, as convincingly as she could. "Listen. There has to be something we can do, something we can figure out. Let me go and talk to your coworker."

Marty shook his head. "You can't. You'll get in trouble."

"I won't get in trouble." Lucy waved a hand. "Also, we need to find a better place to hide you, and I think I know where."

"A treehouse?"

Lucy frowned. "No. The Grand Madrona Hotel! They don't know about you yet, and if I reserve a room for you, they'll never know any better."

He stared at her. "That's a terrible idea."

"It's just for the short term," she said, pulling out her phone. "Whats that guy's name? Marilyn Monroe?"

Marty smirked and shook his head. "David Marilyn."

She typed his name into her phone. The first result was his profile on the company website. "He looks nice."

"He's not that nice, and he's not going to help me."

Lucy drummed her fingers on her chin. "You don't know that. We at least have to try. What other options do we have?"

Marty, who'd taken a seat on the couch and was hanging his head low, popped back up after a moment. "I have no idea, but please don't try to talk to him."

She sighed. "Fine, I won't. But you can't stay here. We need to go, okay? Pack your bag."

He hesitated, but after a moment said, "Fine."

Lucy beamed. She didn't have a full plan yet, but they could figure it out along the way.

Chapter Twenty

Her meeting with Chip came to a natural end when he got an incoming call from a plumber. Claire was able to excuse herself and check her phone. She had a message from Ken – something about dreaming big and acting bigger – and one from Lucy about hotel emails.

It confused her at first, but then she realized what Lucy meant. Claire had access to the hotel's email account, so she acted quickly. Her laptop was in her bag, guarded by Gigi, and she fetched it before settling into a seat in the lobby.

The internet connection was agonizingly slow, but sure enough, there was an email with a warning about Marty. Claire deleted it, cursing the invention of the internet.

They could handle a fax machine, but the internet? No way. People were going to forward that email, print it out, hang it up – heck, the local news might even run with the story. There was no escaping this. Marty was on borrowed time.

They had a meeting set with the espionage attorney, but it was still two weeks away. Claire called the office again, leaving a message to see if there were any cancellations. She stressed that she was available any time, day or night.

Then, as much as it pained her, she forced herself to carry on like normal. She had a meeting with Linda, the events coordinator at the hotel, so Claire packed up her laptop and got back to work.

Their meeting took almost two hours. Linda was a vibrant woman, experienced in hosting events, and clearly didn't want Claire messing up what she had built.

Claire had no intention of causing trouble. The weddings and parties that took place at the hotel were one of the few things that actually made money. They ended their meeting on a good note and Claire found a quiet seat at the hotel bar to check her phone.

She had two messages from Margie. The first said, "The eagle has landed in the nest!" Then, a few minutes later, "AKA I am home. See you again soon?"

Claire shook her head. Margie was a great help, but her spy skills were worse than Marty's. She wrote back, thanking her, and saying she'd be in touch.

There was another nonsensical text from Ken saying he was "ready to see her fly," and a short message from Lucy.

All it said was, "I have a plan."

I have a plan.

Claire liked this message least of all. She called Lucy, but got no answer. Without any meetings for the afternoon, she decided it would be a good time to pay a visit to the cabin.

On her way, Claire called again, but Lucy didn't answer. Claire's mind started churning, and the drive grew longer with every minute Lucy didn't return her call. She was halfway up the driveway when her phone finally rang.

"Hello?"

"Hey Claire! Where are you?"

She let out a sigh. Lucy sounded like herself. "I'm just pulling up to the cabin."

Silence on Lucy's end, then, "Oh."

"Why?"

"Well..." She let out a laugh. "I'm at the hotel again."

Claire got to the top of the driveway and spotted a black sedan. "There's someone here."

"In your car?"

Claire slowed and put the car into park. She could make out two heads through the back window. "No, at the cabin. Where's...? You know."

"With me. I'm getting a room for – er, me."

"*Lucy,*" Claire whispered. She watched as Agent McCoy and Agent Alvarez got out of the car and started walking toward her.

"Something had to be done! There were visitors at the cabin earlier and – well, you know, I don't like visitors."

"Uh huh." Claire forced a smile and waved at them. "I'm about to talk to them now."

"Yikes!" Lucy dropped her voice. "Good luck."

"Thanks." Claire let out a sigh and ended the call before opening her car door.

"Hey there," Agent Alvarez called out.

Claire swung her legs out of the car, pulling her bag behind her. "Hi."

"In a hurry, Miss Cooke?" Agent McCoy asked, crossing his arms.

She wanted to be careful with her replies. "It's a busy time for me, Agent McCoy."

He smiled, following her to the front door. "We won't take up much of your day. Do you mind if we have a chat?"

Claire was just about to unlock the door. She stopped herself, putting her keys back into her purse. "Sure. What can I do for you?"

Agent Alvarez flashed a smile at her. "How about we go inside and have a seat?"

Aha. Claire had spent far too many years working with lawyers to fall for that one. All the agents needed was to catch a glimpse of something suspicious inside the cabin and they'd be able to get a warrant to do a search. She was not interested in that. "Let's not," she said. "It's a mess in there."

Agent McCoy took a step closer. "We don't mind."

"We can stay out here and chat," she said with a smile.

The smile faded from Agent McCoy's face. "I'm getting worried about you, Miss Cooke."

Claire raised an eyebrow. He didn't look worried. He looked scary. She wondered what he had on her. Not enough to get a warrant. At least, not yet.

"Why is that?" she asked.

He let out a heavy sigh. "Because I know you're keeping a secret. I know it's weighing on you."

She frowned. This guy would be a great psychic. He was quite convincing. "I don't think you know much about me, Agent McCoy."

"Oh, I think I do." He took a step closer. "This is the last chance I can give you. Talk to us now. Let us help you. Don't let yourself be duped by a con man."

Claire was only inches away from him, studying the lines in his face. He was older than his partner. Surely he'd seen a lot. She appreciated that he was convinced she was in trouble.

If only she could tell him the truth.

If only he'd believe it.

Agent Alvarez cleared his throat. "Please, Claire. We want to help."

He was looking at her much more sympathetically. It didn't seem like an act to Claire. He seemed like a sweet guy.

She gave him a half smile in return. "Like I said before, I will contact you if there's anything I can do to help you."

"Tell me, Claire," Agent Alvarez said in a low voice. "Are you in danger?"

Oh, bless him. She shook her head. "I am not. Thank you, gentlemen, but I have to run."

As much as she didn't approve of Lucy's plan – or being left out of it – Claire was now quite thankful for her quick thinking.

She smiled at them both before slipping into the darkness of the cabin.

Chapter Twenty-one

A week passed and Lucy couldn't help but marvel that her scheme of hiding Marty in plain sight was working. True, he was getting a bit antsy, and housekeeping wouldn't stop asking about coming in to clean. But, other than that, it was going swimmingly.

The local news had picked up the story about the possible fugitive on the island, and though people became more aware of it, no one seemed to actually think it was true. It was more of a "Isn't that funny?" sort of thing, which Lucy was happy to encourage any chance she got.

Claire remained concerned, but from Lucy's perspective, it seemed like the people of Orcas Island had a hard time believing that a so-called criminal could live among them.

Criminal. What a joke. Lucy was confident that Marty's name would be cleared as soon as they got a chance to talk to the attorney Claire had found. She'd gotten his name from her old coworker – the now Attorney General – and he was the best. If anyone could save Marty, it was him.

The only problem with being the best, however, was that he was busy. They still had another week to wait before they could meet with him.

It all seemed silly to Lucy, especially if Marty's old coworker could clear things up. Why spend thousands of dollars on an attorney when a conversation with an old friend could do the trick?

That was, at least, what she told herself when she first found David Marilyn's dating profile. She hadn't been *looking* for him, but he'd appeared nevertheless.

It was all by chance, really. Out of boredom one night when she and Marty were watching *Love It or List It* at the hotel, she'd updated her location on her dating profile to the Seattle area.

It wasn't her fault that the algorithm showed her David Marilyn, or that she recognized him, or that when she sent him a wink he messaged her back within a few hours.

They'd chatted, and he asked her out. What was she supposed to say? *No?*

That would be spitting in the face of fate, and of dating algorithms. Who was Lucy to do such a thing?

Their date was set for Wednesday night – drinks at a bar for an early happy hour. A very noncommittal sort of date, and Lucy appreciated that David must be a pro. There was no need to subject themselves to a full dinner together if they didn't hit it off at first – or if David didn't want to talk about Marty.

Lucy took the express ferry to the mainland on Wednesday morning, allowing plenty of time before her date. There was no chance she'd let something as annoying as the weather or rough seas ruin her hopes of saving Marty.

She told no one her plan. That way, if it failed, they didn't have to worry about it. Instead, she'd claimed to have a job interview. The perfect cover.

Lucy got to the bar early and scoped out a seat with some privacy. There weren't many options, though, so she decided that the end of the bar would have to do.

As she waited, she reviewed David's profile again. It said he liked golf, baseball, and sunsets. Lucy was more of a group fitness and sunrise kind of girl, but perhaps opposites would attract?

David arrived a few minutes early, waving when he spotted her.

"Lucy?" he asked, approaching with his hand outstretched.

She accepted his handshake and smiled. "Hi, David. It's good to meet you."

"You look nice," he said, before adding, "absolutely stunning."

"Oh, thank you," she said. "You look nice, too."

He ran a hand near his stiffly gelled hair. "Yeah, baby!"

Ah. An Austin Powers impression. Not a good one, but it was the thought that counted.

They took their seats. He was a cute guy. Maybe a little nerdy, but Lucy liked nerds. As long as they weren't condescending.

"What are you drinking?" he asked, pulling a menu toward them.

She tapped her chin. "I had my eye on the cranberry sangria."

"I don't hold alcohol well myself, so I might just start with the soda."

"Oh!" Lucy flipped the menu over to look at the non-alcoholic options. "I'll get a soda too, then."

"It's not that I don't drink," he said. "It's that I shouldn't drink."

Lucy wasn't sure how to respond to that. She had plenty of friends who didn't do well with alcohol, and she didn't even like drinking all that much herself.

If he'd felt that way, though, perhaps he shouldn't have suggested a bar for their date?

He didn't wait for her response. "I mean, I do drink, but I tend to go too far. You know, throwing up, peeing in public, the works. I'll save that for our second date."

Charming. "Got it."

He put in an order for a cherry coke, and Lucy asked for a root beer float. It was still a night out – she needed to have a little fun.

After their drinks arrived, he turned to her. "So, what do you do?"

That was always a hard question for her. "I'm sort of between jobs right now. I've done a lot of different things, but I'm trying to figure out what I'm really interested in."

He shook his head. "Not me. I've always known what I wanted to do. My parents got me a computer when I was nine and my mom always says that was when I just blossomed."

Lucy tried not to frown. How come she'd never blossomed? "You work with computers?"

"You could say that," he said with a smile. "I went to school for computer engineering with a double major in computer science. Now I work at a startup."

"Neat. I worked at startup once. It was sort of chaotic, but we had a lot of fun before it all fell apart."

He sat back, crossing his arms. "The startup where I work isn't going to fall apart."

Go on. "Oh?"

He took a sip of his cherry coke. "We're developing a proprietary technology and it's going *very* well."

Lucy tried to feign surprise. "That's cool."

He then launched into a twenty-minute story about his interests leading up to his position in the company, what he worked on in college, and that he graduated magna cum laude.

Just in case she had the audacity to think he wasn't impressive, he explained to her that his GPA was considered phenomenal at his school, whereas at a state school it wouldn't have been considered as impressive.

Lucy muted her thoughts. If he'd asked her, he would've found out that she'd gone to a state school and not graduated, honors or otherwise.

He did not ask her anything, however, and eventually steered himself back to talking about his current company.

"We have the best client on the line – the government – and it looks like our parent company might be selling, too."

"Oh no," she said flatly.

"No, it'll actually be amazing. I own stock in the company and it's going to go nuts."

"I thought you said that the government was your buyer."

He nodded. "Oh, I see how you could be confused. They're going to buy the product, not the company. They're going to license it. It's better this way, because they're paying every year to use it. It's brilliant, really."

She forced a smile. "Sounds like it."

"We're about to be bought out by a venture-capital firm out of New York – Steel and Steal. Have you heard of them?"

Lucy shook her head. "Can't say that I have."

He described, in detail, what it meant for his stock portfolio.

Lucy didn't know how to buy stocks, nor did she have any interest in learning. Her mind began to wander, and she couldn't believe she was actually wishing he'd talk about golf instead.

She tuned back into the conversation when he said, "I'm pretty good with money, but even I couldn't have expected this."

Lucy cleared her throat. "What's the program called? The one you're developing."

"SureFired," he said, pushing his empty glass away, shooting a nod at the bartender. "It's a wildfire prediction algorithm."

All the talking must have made him quite thirsty. Lucy took her chance to speak, knowing it might not come again. "That sounds familiar. I think I know someone who worked on that."

"Really? That'd be surprising."

Such a charmer. "Yeah, his name is Marty. Marty Coursin? Do you know him?"

The smile dropped from David's face. He pulled back, his posture growing rigid. "Never heard of him."

Shoot. Maybe that was the wrong way to do it, but she was getting desperate. They'd been there over an hour and she'd hardly said more than ten sentences.

"Really?" Lucy cocked her head to the side. "Maybe he was working on a different program that did the same thing. It sounded like the same sort of technology, you know? I feel like I've heard about that before."

David shrugged. "Maybe."

Lucy needed to do some damage control. "That's really cool, though. You're working on something that can save lives."

He nodded, but said nothing.

Terrific. Suddenly the guy who couldn't stop talking didn't have anything else to say.

After a few minutes, he announced that he'd had a nice time, but it was time for him to go. "It was a pleasure meeting you. We should do this again," he said as he paid for his cherry soda.

Lucy didn't fail to notice that Mr. Moneybags did not offer to pay for her root beer float.

"Yeah, that'd be nice," she said, returning his lie.

He left her there, poking at her ice cream, as he stepped out of the restaurant to place a call.

Chapter Twenty-two

"Who do you think she's hiding in there?" asked Gigi.

Chip looked up from the computer screen. "What?"

"In room 106."

He'd just finished running an antivirus program. Gigi insisted she hadn't downloaded anything, and yet, after he'd removed fifteen viruses, the computer miraculously started working again. "Lucy is staying in that room."

"No way." She lowered her voice. "Lucy isn't staying in there. I hardly ever see her."

"She's probably out sightseeing all day."

Gigi shook her head. "Layla and I think Claire is hiding a secret sweetheart in there."

Chip felt a flare of annoyance, but he didn't want to show it. It was his own fault they were talking like this. He never should've let the staff treat Claire with snark at the beginning. Now he couldn't get it under control. "I don't think so."

"I saw Claire carrying food in, and trash out, so –"

"That's enough." He turned to face her. "Do you want to lose your job? Is this how you treat your boss?"

Gigi laughed. "Don't be jealous, Chip."

He paused. How could Gigi have known that he'd be jealous of Claire having a sweetheart? Was he *that* obvious?

Gigi let out a sigh. "We make stuff up about you, too. You just aren't that interesting most of the time."

Oh. That kind of jealous. "You caught me."

Gigi mused on. "I swear I heard a man's voice in there the other day."

"Isn't your shift over soon?"

She looked at her watch and perked up. "It is! Time flies when you're having fun. Addie should be here any minute."

As happy as Gigi would be to see Addie, Chip would be twice as happy. Addie was much nicer than Gigi. He was seriously considering putting her on the day shift. "Gigi, we have a photographer coming in on Friday to take new pictures of the hotel. Please treat her kindly when she gets here. Her name is Morgan."

Gigi smiled. "Sure thing, boss man."

Chip went back to his office and made some calls. After that, he even found the strength to update all of the revenue sheets. That was one of his least favorite things to do, and he usually put it off.

Now, thanks to his need to avoid thinking about whom Claire had in room 106, the revenue sheets were caught up from the last four months.

An email rolled in from one of the contractors with a quote for replacing the bathroom tile and tubs. Claire was right. It was far less expensive than redoing the entirety of the bathrooms. She'd be excited to see it. He sent her a text message to see if she was busy.

"Just grabbing some dinner before getting back to the hotel tonight. Don't wait up for me! We can talk about it tomorrow," she wrote back.

Nonsense. He didn't mind waiting. There was nothing for him at home. At the hotel, he had work to do, people to yell at, rooms to check on...

No. He wasn't going to feed into Gigi's gossip. He knew that Lucy was staying in that room. He'd seen her go in and out. Or, at least, he thought he had.

If anyone had a secret sweetheart, it was Lucy. Maybe she was hiding it from Claire. That made the most sense.

Except...it didn't make sense for Lucy to hide anyone in her mom's hotel. She could have picked literally any other hotel on the island.

He frowned. Somehow the rest of his work didn't seem that appealing. Chip walked out into the lobby, checking in with the bar and restaurant staff – they had no complaints. Business as usual.

Addie was at the front desk, talking to a guest and smiling. Actually smiling. What a nice image that was for the hotel. Chip nodded at her as he walked by, and she waved him down.

"Hey, I have something here," she said once the guest stepped away.

He drummed his fingers on the counter. "What's up?"

Addie knelt down, reappearing with a scarf. "Someone lost this in the lobby and hasn't come back to claim it. Is it okay if I email the guests a picture of it?"

Chip took the rough material into his hand. "I think I know whose scarf this is."

"Oh, really?" Addie smiled. "Great!"

"Thanks, Addie." Chip tossed it over his shoulder.

It could be Lucy's scarf. No, he was quite certain it was hers. He'd just swing by her room and drop it off.

Chapter Twenty-three

Claire managed to sneak into the hotel through one of the back doors unnoticed. She and Marty were just settling in to eat fish and chips when there was a knock at the door.

Claire instinctively pulled out her phone to see if Lucy had forgotten her key, but there was no message from her. She still hadn't written back to tell her how her interview had gone.

She whispered "let me go see who this is" to Marty. He nodded and quietly moved out of sight of the door.

Through the peephole, Claire could see Chip standing there in a flattering navy sweater. Butterflies fluttered in her chest.

"Hi," she said, slipping out of the door and closing it behind her.

"Oh, Claire. I didn't know you were in," he said with a smile.

"Yeah, just, you know, brought Lucy something to eat." He didn't answer right away, and Claire had the urge to keep talking. "She's not feeling well, had an interview on the mainland, you know – just, yeah."

He frowned. "I'm sorry to hear that. Is there anything I can do?"

Claire shook her head. "No, but thank you."

"Well – someone lost a scarf in the lobby. I thought it might be Lucy's?"

He held it up and Claire looked it over – an ugly, sad looking thing, with fraying ends and snags throughout. Not something that fashion-forward Lucy would ever touch. "I don't think so, but thanks for thinking of her."

"Do you think she'd like to see it, just in case?"

Claire shook her head. "No, I'm pretty sure it's not hers."

He stood there, looking at her, seemingly hesitating. A paranoid thought crossed her mind – that he was onto her, that he knew what she was doing...

"Lovely weather we're having, huh?" she said, hating herself as soon as the words left her lips.

"Oh yeah. It was nice to have a break from the rain."

"Normally I like rain. It's nice, in a way. I like the sound of the raindrops on the cabin roof." She cleared her throat. "Any news on the menu for the Valentine's Day dinner?"

He looked up, thinking. "You know, I'm not sure. I'll have to check on that."

"Okay. Great. Well...."

He nodded. "I'll get going, then. Are we meeting tomorrow? I got some numbers from the contractor."

She fidgeted with her hair. "Oh sure, any time. How about ten?"

"Sure, yeah, that works for me."

He took a step back, and Claire was about to turn and open the door behind her when something caught her eye. Just over Chip's shoulder she saw Lucy's distinct green hat, bobbing down the hallway.

She wanted to give Lucy a signal, something to tell her to run – or at least to turn around!

But it was too late. Lucy spotted her and started waving, yelling out, "I made it back!"

Chip spun around, the surprise evident on his face. "Hi, Lucy."

Claire needed this interaction to be over. "I was just waiting for you, Lucy. I got fish and chips."

Lucy let out a long breath. "That sounds great. I've had a *day*."

Chip locked his gaze onto her. "That's a heavy meal. You must be feeling better."

She waved a hand, unwinding a scarf from around her neck. "I feel better to be back." She eyed the scarf in his hands. "Ew. What is that?"

"A lost scarf," he said, holding it forward. "I thought it might be yours."

Lucy made a face. "Absolutely not, and I'm kind of insulted you thought that."

Claire forced a smile. "We'd better eat before the food gets cold."

"Right." Lucy nodded, pulling out her room key and opening the door. "See you later, Chip."

"See you," he said. He was about to walk away when he stopped himself. "I thought she was already here?"

He knows. *He knows.* "No, no. I knew she was on her way."

"Ah."

They stared at each other for a moment, Claire feeling the sweat forming on her back. She hated lying. She was about to speak again when Chip's phone rang.

He excused himself. "It's Chip."

Claire watched his face as he listened intently.

"No, Addie, that's okay." He switched ears. "Of course, you should rent them a room. We have nothing to hide."

Her stomach tightened. That didn't sound good.

Chip let out a sigh. "They can request a room but not to be next to a particular guest. You know what, I'm still here. I'll stop by."

Once he hung up, she asked, "Is everything okay?"

He scratched his head. "Those FBI agents are back, at the front desk. Making requests, apparently. That's one thing Gigi is good for."

Claire let out a nervous laugh. "The FBI?"

"No. Denying requests." He started walking down the hall.

Claire followed. "I'll come with you."

They walked in silence until they reached the lobby.

Agent McCoy waved when he saw her. "Miss Cooke. I didn't expect to see you here so late."

She flashed a smile. "How are you, gentleman?"

"We're doing well," Agent Alvarez said. "Enjoying our time on the island."

Addie spoke, her voice small. "They asked for a list of all of the guests."

"Just to make sure we're not staying next to any criminals," Agent McCoy said, winking at Claire.

She was getting sick of this guy. He had nothing on her, but he wouldn't stop poking around, trying to rattle her.

Claire smiled back. "That's not a service that we offer, unfortunately. You can try one of the other resorts on the island, or perhaps on the mainland?"

He let out a laugh. "No, I think we'll stay here for a bit. I like the views."

Claire walked around the front desk and Addie stepped aside. "One room or two?"

McCoy and Alvarez looked at each other, then Agent Alvarez spoke. "Two, please."

Claire clicked around on the computer, finding what she needed. "We have two side-by-side rooms available."

"What floor are they on?"

She pretended to look at the screen, though she knew exactly where she was going to put them. "The third floor."

"I'm afraid of heights," Agent McCoy said. "What about the second floor?"

She nodded, clicking through again. "We have two rooms across the hall from each other."

He shook his head. "Actually, first floor might be best."

"All booked up, I'm afraid," she said, stare unbroken. "Second floor, then?"

He pulled out his wallet and slid a credit card across the desk. "Please."

She managed to complete the booking without any help. It was her first time doing it start to finish, but her pride was overshadowed by the gravity of the situation.

Once she handed them their room keys, they walked off and got onto the elevator.

"Thanks Addie," Claire said, flashing a smile. "Let me know if they have any other issues."

Addie nodded. "Of course!"

For some reason, Claire found it impossible to look Chip in the eye. She started walking down the hall, calling out, "Sorry, I'd better get back."

"Actually," Chip said, gently catching her on the shoulder. "Can I talk to you in my office for a minute?"

Butterflies again. Maybe she could tell him. Maybe he already knew?

"Sure," she said weakly.

She walked ahead this time, waiting as he unlocked the door, then going in and standing near his desk.

"What was that about?" he asked, closing the door behind him.

Claire shook her head. "It's a misunderstanding."

"I would like to understand," Chip said, voice low. "You need to start telling me things."

"I can't," she said, almost in a whisper. "Not yet at least. I want to, but..."

"Then tell me why that guy looked like he was ready to pounce on you."

She let out a sigh. "He's just a jerk. I guess he's the mean one. Agent Alvarez is a much better listener."

Chip sat down, rubbing his face in his hands. "Can you at least tell me who is staying in room 106?"

Claire had to unclench her jaw. "Lucy is staying there, Chip. You know that."

He shook his head. "Don't lie to me, Claire. Please don't lie to me."

Her heart sank. Even she hadn't believed that last one. Her voice was weak. No, her entire delivery was weak. She hated the way he was looking at her. She wanted his warm smile, his deep laugh. She needed him to forgive her.

"Please, if you just give me some time, it'll make sense."

He studied her for a moment. "Come on, Claire. I believed in you. I believed you when you told me that we were partners, and that we were working together. I thought I could trust you."

"You can, I just –"

"Can I?" He stopped himself, letting out a heavy breath. "I feel like you're hiding something. And we've got the FBI poking around the hotel. I mean – what's going on?"

Claire felt like she was on the brink of tears. Everything was falling apart around her.

Still, she couldn't cry in front of him. She squeaked out an "I'm sorry, Chip," before pulling the office door open and rushing back to room 106.

Chapter Twenty-four

What had happened to Claire? That long exchange in front of the door made Marty nervous. As Lucy debated whether Claire would come back for her fish and chips, Marty quietly packed his bag.

"Did she say that she got one for me, or that we were going to split it? Because it looks pretty big," Lucy said, eyeing the generous portion of fried fish.

Marty shrugged, packing up his toiletries. It was nice having a bathroom for a while. He was going to miss that. "I don't know. You can have mine if you want."

"I'm not going to take yours," she said, looking up at him. "Hang on. Are you going somewhere?"

"If I need to, yes."

"Why?"

He shot a look at the door. "I'm not sure what happened to Claire, but I think Chip is getting suspicious."

Lucy crossed her arms. "You're way too stressed out. Relax. Everything's fine. Claire's probably just talking to Chip because she has a crush on him."

Marty paused. "You think Claire has a crush on Chip?"

"Oh yeah. Big time." Lucy popped the top off the tartar sauce container. "She's always telling me all these stories about him, and whenever he comes around, she gets excited and her eyes light up."

Marty considered this for a moment. He'd noticed that Claire was nice to Chip, but she was nice to everyone. If anyone would know if Claire liked the guy, though, it was Lucy.

"Maybe you're right. I just need to be ready to run. Being in here..." He let out a sigh. His eyes felt heavy, and his shoulders were sore from sitting on the bed all day. "I'm getting stir crazy."

Lucy smiled at him. "I don't blame you, but try not to worry. We'll meet with the attorney next week and figure everything out."

Marty nodded. It helped to have someone to bounce his fears onto. After spending so many hours alone in this room, he felt like he was going mad.

He was also sick of talking about himself. "How was your interview?" he asked. "Do you think you'll like the job?"

"Well..." Lucy bit her lip and narrowed her eyes. "It wasn't so much an interview as it was a date."

He raised his eyebrows. "Oh. Why did you say it was an interview?"

"It's just, you know." She took a bite of the fried fish. "It's not a big deal, but the date was with someone you know."

"Someone I know?" He thought on this for a moment, but he couldn't think of any friends they had in common.

Lucy took a sip of soda before quickly adding, "It was David Marilyn."

"What?" Marty stood up. "Please don't tell me that you tried to talk to him."

"Not exactly. He's kind of hard to talk to," Lucy said. "I could hardly get a word in. The guy is in love with himself."

Marty smiled. "Yeah, that's Dave."

Lucy stuffed some french fries into her mouth. "I get what you meant now, about him not being the answer."

"I'm glad you didn't talk about me to him," Marty said, shaking his head. "That would've been a disaster."

"I mean...I *mentioned* that I knew you, and then all of a sudden, he didn't want to talk anymore."

Marty stared at her. "Lucy..."

"I know, I should've listened to you. It's not a big deal, though. It was just a bad date."

"But if you were asking about me –"

She waved a hand. "He doesn't even really know who I am. I just said that I knew you. He was the one who brought up SureFired," she said, taking another bite. "He was blabbing on and on. He said that his stock options look great, and that they're going to save lives and –"

"Hm." Marty sat back down. "So you didn't ask him to prove that I'm innocent or anything?"

"Of course not." Lucy let out a sigh. "You were right. He wasn't helpful at all."

The room door opened and Marty instinctively darted behind a wall.

"Hi Lucy," Claire's voice called out.

The door clicked shut and Claire came into view.

Lucy gave her a hug, then pulled away and looked at Claire's face. "What's wrong? Were you crying?"

Claire shook her head and let out a breath. "It's nothing. We just had some issues with the hotel."

"What kind of issues?" asked Marty, stomach sinking.

Claire frowned. "I don't want to worry you, but it's those two FBI agents again. They decided they wanted to stay at the hotel."

Marty grabbed his bag and swung the strap over his shoulder. "I have to go."

"Hang on," Lucy said, grabbing his arm. "They don't know that you're here, right?"

"They seem to be getting pretty close," Marty said.

"Where are you going to go?" asked Lucy. "How are you going to do it without them spotting you?"

He shrugged. "I don't know, but it's not safe to stay here."

Claire put her hands on her hips. "I may not be any good at owning a hotel, but I will keep you safe, Marty."

For the first time since she'd walked back in the room, Marty had a chance to really look at Claire. Her eyes were red, and there was a smudge of black makeup under her eyes. She had been crying.

She didn't deserve to have this stress on her. He needed to go.

"Look," he said softly, "I appreciate everything you've done for me, but I can't stay here and get you in trouble. I just can't."

"You are not getting me in trouble," Claire said firmly. "Sit down and eat your dinner."

A laugh burst out of Lucy. "Oh, now you're getting it."

Marty felt the urge to laugh, too, at the absurdity of it all. Lucy had run off to Seattle, lying to Claire and him, to go on a date with David, but now Marty was the one getting in trouble!

The only sensible thing would be for him to leave them both in peace, but they refused. It was infuriating.

He watched as Claire wandered around the room – to the desk, then back to the front door, then taking a seat on a chair before speaking again. "I still don't think that they have any information about you or me. Otherwise, they'd have a search warrant and they'd find you quickly."

"That's true, but I can't stay and –"

Claire shook her head. "No." Her voice was soft, but firm. "You'll stay here. I'll keep an eye on them. We'll see the attorney soon, and we'll figure everything out. Together."

Marty didn't know what else to say. Lucy thrust a box of fish and chips into his hands and started telling them about how she'd almost missed the ferry.

Family made no sense sometimes. He sat back and took a bite of fish.

It took less than fifteen hours for their plan to fall apart.

After the fish was gone and the last fry was eaten, Claire retired to a room across the hall from Marty's, while Lucy stayed in one next to the elevators for better visibility. Since it was her second room at the hotel, she had to make up a name and settled on Marilyn Monroe, in an apparent jab at David.

Marty wasn't able to sleep. He laid in bed, restlessly flipping and turning, listening to every sound. Every hour or so he'd get up and peek through the window, sure that he'd catch sight of an FBI team circling the building.

He never saw anything out of place, but more than once, as he stared out into the darkness, he considered trying to slip away. Claire would be upset, but she'd understand. The real issue was that the window was stuck. Even when he'd tried to crack it for some fresh air, it wouldn't budge.

Marty gave up, and around six that morning, finally drifted off to sleep. He was deep in a dream when there was a knock at his door.

He jolted awake, heart racing, grabbing his bag before peering into the peephole.

"Housekeeping!" a voice called out.

The adrenaline was making him nauseated. He cleared his throat and raised his voice, trying to sound like Lucy. "No thank you!"

It was a poor imitation, but the woman moved on. Marty stood there, staring out of the peephole for a minute before making up his mind.

This whole thing was ridiculous. He couldn't spend another day locked up in this hotel room with two FBI agents breathing down his neck. Claire didn't deserve to have her hotel go down the drain over him. Lucy certainly didn't need to get any other sweet but misguided ideas about how to help him.

Marty threw on his jacket and returned to the window, peering around the edge of the curtain.

It didn't look like anything was going on, and there wasn't a soul outside. He undid the lock and forced the window open, pushing so hard part of the frame cracked under the force.

He didn't care. The window was finally releasing him, so he climbed out, landing with a thud on the grass below. With the hood of his jacket popped over his head, he quickly moved toward the road.

There was no one waiting for him outside, no team dressed in black, no helicopters, and no scent dogs. It was just him, the birds, and the boats off in the distance.

Maybe he had overreacted. Marty's shoulders relaxed the further he got from the hotel. It wasn't until he was walking alongside the parking lot, hiding amongst the trees, that he saw something unusual. A black SUV had pulled up to the front door of the hotel, unloading six men before pulling away.

The hair stood up on Marty's neck. Was this it? Was it really happening? Or had he finally lost his mind?

He wasn't going to wait around to find out. Marty picked up his pace, keeping his head down, and promptly walked into the side of a truck.

"Do you mind telling me why you just busted one of my windows?" said a voice.

Marty looked up, peering into the open window of the truck. The guy looked angry – annoyed, even – but he didn't look like FBI.

"Sorry," Marty said hurriedly, trying to walk around, keeping his head down.

The truck lurched forward. "Not so fast."

Marty looked up, just in time to see a second black SUV arrive and unload another six men into the hotel.

The driver of the truck turned to see what Marty was looking at. "Friends of yours?" he asked.

Marty felt a panic setting in. He was having a hard time breathing and was seeing spots. He shook his head.

The driver of the truck frowned. "Are you...Lucy's friend?"

Maybe this guy was FBI? That would be clever – flush him out of the room, then have him walk right into the arms of an agent... "Never heard of her."

"Listen kid, I'm the manager of the hotel whose window you just broke. If you try to run off, I'll call the police."

Another SUV came rolling through, and Marty ducked low so he wasn't spotted. Once they passed, he leaned into the truck window. "You're Chip?"

"The one and only."

Marty felt like he was going to throw up. The newest carload had unloaded, these agents running to the side of the hotel. They were getting into place. "You're the one Claire likes."

Chip cocked his head to the side. "What?"

"Give me a ride. Please. Let me in." He tried the door handle, but it was locked.

Chip shook his head. "You're out of your mind."

"If you don't help me, Claire's going to be arrested."

Chip scowled at him, but a moment later he unlocked the doors. "Get in."

Chapter Twenty-five

The kid got in and Chip started to drive. He was about to ask him a question when his phone rang.

"It's Chip," he said.

"Chip! It's Gigi." Her voice was hushed. "The FBI is here and they're doing a raid! Everyone is supposed to stay where they are."

"Did they tell you why?"

"No, but I'm calling you because Ken is here and he's refusing to follow their orders. I think he's going to get arrested."

Chip smiled. "That'd be too bad."

"Oh, they're yelling at me. Gotta go."

He rushed to add, "Are you going to –"

It was too late. She'd ended the call.

Chip shot a look at the kid in his passenger seat. He wasn't really a kid. He looked young to Chip, but he was probably older than his son. It dawned on him that he might be dangerous.

"I just got a call that a bunch of FBI agents are in my hotel. Are they looking for you?"

He shifted, clutching his bag. "Yes."

What was in that bag? Chip had heard there was some talks of the FBI looking for someone on the islands, but he hadn't paid it any attention. Now he wished he had.

"Why is that?" Chip asked.

The kid said nothing.

Chip continued driving, leaving the hotel behind. He decided to try something else. "Why would Claire get arrested?"

It took him a moment to reply. "Because of me."

No kidding. Chip resisted the urge to roll his eyes. They were getting nowhere. "If you don't start talking, I'm going to turn around and hand you in. Is that what you want?"

The kid leaned down, and for a second Chip was afraid he would pull a weapon from his bag.

He didn't, though. Instead, he buried his face in his hands. "Maybe that's a good idea. I don't know."

What kind of a criminal was this kid? He wasn't a good negotiator. "Was Claire helping you?"

"I don't want her to get in trouble."

"I'm not going to rat her out," Chip said heavily. "Now talk."

He let out a sigh. "She wanted to get me to a lawyer."

Chip nodded. "Okay. And?"

"We were supposed to meet with him next week. I don't know how they found me."

Chip drove along in silence. They'd already reached Olga, the sleepy little town where he lived. He'd driven there instinctively, but now he wasn't sure what to do with the young outlaw. His gut told him that the kid wasn't a threat.

"What's your name, kid?"

"Marty. Marty Coursin."

Chip turned onto the road that led to his house. It was deserted, and quiet, the tall trees whispering in the breeze above them. He pulled up to the house, putting his truck into park. None of his neighbors were outside, so there was no risk of being pulled into chit chat.

"Let's go, Marty," Chip said as he got out of the truck.

Marty followed without a word. Chip unlocked the back door to the house and motioned for the fugitive – or was he his captive now? – to go inside.

Marty did as instructed, taking a seat at the kitchen table.

Chip closed the door behind him. He needed to maintain some aura of authority, even if the little punk scared him. "Let me see some ID."

Marty reached into his pants pocket, then his jacket pockets. "Oh no."

"What?"

Marty frowned, unzipping his bag. "I think I forgot my wallet."

Chip crossed his arms. "Where?"

"Back at the hotel! They're going to find it! It'll be proof that I was there."

"Hang on, back it up. How do you know Claire?"

Marty didn't look up from his search of the bag. "I'm her nephew."

A wave of relief washed over Chip. Her nephew. He thought the guy looked a little young to be Claire's date, but what did he know? She was an heiress after all.

Actually, her fortune was even more reason for an unscrupulous person to come after her. "Her nephew? But..." He trailed off. There was no way. Claire never mentioned a nephew.

Marty sat back and looked at Chip. "I can tell you the story, but you won't believe me."

Chip took a seat at the table across from Marty. "Try me."

Marty talked nonstop for the next half hour. It was a long story, and a wild one – one that Chip wasn't apt to believe. Of course, a con man would show up at Claire's doorstep after she inherited millions of dollars, claiming to be related to her. It was the perfect plan.

"What proof do you have, Marty? Of any of this?"

Marty shrugged. "Ask Claire. She'll tell you. I gave her a picture of my mom holding me after I was born."

Chip crossed his arms. "And you just decided to show up one day? Conveniently after you heard she bought the hotel."

"No, it wasn't like that." Marty shook his head. "I didn't know I was adopted until a few weeks ago. I thought Claire was my mom. I had nowhere else to go."

Chip stared at him. "Why?"

"Because I tried to do the right thing and I was set up as a Chinese spy."

"You're one heck of a storyteller, kid," Chip said, standing up to get himself some water. He considered offering some to Marty, but he didn't want to seem too friendly.

Marty shrugged. "You asked. That's the truth. Claire did nothing wrong. She wanted to help me. She insisted on it."

Chip took a swig of water and stared at him. That, at least, checked out. He sat back down. "Why do they think you're a spy?"

He leaned forward. "How much do you know about wild-fires?"

"Enough, I think."

Marty reached into his bag and pulled out a pad of paper and a pen. He started writing, "Fuel, heat transfer, conduction. Moisture levels. Topography. Wind." He drew lines between the words, listing more beneath each.

Chip watched intently, listening as Marty explained the wildfire model he helped create. For the first time in their conversation, Chip had no doubt that what Marty was telling him was true. The kid was an expert, speaking quickly and passionately about the program he'd help develop.

"Sounds pretty cool, Marty," Chip said, studying the paper in front of him.

"It was cool." Marty sat back. "Except no one wanted to give us the time to perfect it."

"Perfect what? The program?"

Marty nodded. "Yeah – SureFired. They wanted to sell it to the highest bidder as fast as they could. That's where the prob-lems started."

Chip listened with increasing discomfort as Marty described a scenario that Chip was far too familiar with – profit over people.

Except in this story, unlike in his own, Marty chose to do the right thing. He had chosen to speak up.

Though Chip forever regretted not trying to do something about what he'd seen before the economic crash, he'd never considered what it would've meant for his career. He would've lost everything.

Not that it mattered. He'd lost everything anyway.

But would the bank have gone after him and framed him, the way that Marty claimed he was being framed? It never occurred to Chip before, but he could see it. Whistleblowers ended up in jail cells more often than not.

Marty kept talking, and as Chip listened, he pulled out his phone. He wasn't so worried about letting his guard down any more. Marty was the least threatening fugitive he'd ever known. It didn't hurt that he looked like Claire.

Chip searched for "SureFired," pulling up an article about the company being eyed by a buyer – Steel and Steal. Chip laughed out loud.

Marty leaned forward. "Did you hear from Claire?"

"No, unfortunately not. I just found SureFired's buyer. Steel and Steal."

"Oh." Marty shifted in his seat. "Yeah, they were in talks for a while. They wanted to see the contract with the feds go through. I guess it finally did."

"I know these guys," Chip said, standing up. "Well, Steel Montgomery in particular. I worked with him for years. He's ruthless."

Marty hung his head. "I don't doubt it."

Chip's phone rang again and he ignored it, instead getting a glass of water for Marty. "What's your plan, kid? If everything you told me was true, then what are you going to do about it?"

"I don't know." He accepted the glass. "I don't know what to do. I've been running for my life."

Chip studied him. If he really were a Chinese spy, Chip thought they would've saved him by now, whisking him away to a lab in the mountains to reproduce this technology for their own use.

His phone dinged – a voicemail. He let out a sigh. "Hang on a second."

Chip hit play, holding the phone to his ear. It was Gigi again. "This is so crazy," her voice mused, letting out a giggle. "Ken got arrested because he wouldn't listen, and you'll never guess – *Lucy* got arrested too! All this time I thought that it was Claire, but it must've been Lucy. The guests are freaked out, though, so tell me what you want me to do. I told them it was a gas leak, but they're not buying it."

Chip shut his eyes.

"What happened?" asked Marty.

"Lucy's been arrested."

The color drained from Marty's face. "This is all my fault."

"It does seem that way." Chip said, offering a weak smile.

Marty finished the water and stood. "All right. I'm going to turn myself in and see if I can get Lucy released. I don't have any other options."

Chip had just had an idea. "Hang on. I've got...a plan."

Chapter Twenty-six

T he world unraveled in a matter of seconds, and Claire didn't even see it coming. She was at the front desk talking to Gigi about a guest complaint when Agent McCoy strolled over.

"I'm really enjoying my stay here," he said with a smile.

Claire smiled back. "That's nice to hear."

"I was surprised the judge issued a warrant as fast as he did," he said, helping himself to a mint. "Made me glad that I stayed on site."

Claire didn't know how to respond to that. "I'm sorry?"

He pulled a sheet of paper out of his pocket. "This is a search warrant for room 106."

Oh no. So they'd finally gotten something – enough for a warrant. She stared at it, unable to absorb any of the words on the page.

"I'm going to hang out here with you, if you don't mind. I wouldn't want you to do anything silly, like trying to warn her."

Claire narrowed her eyes. "Her?"

"Okay Miss Cooke," he said, taking the warrant back. "That's enough pretending."

A second later, federal agents poured into the lobby. They moved wordlessly, rushing past the front desk and down the hall toward room 106.

Claire went to follow them, but Agent McCoy grabbed her by the shoulder and pulled her back. "No, no. You stay here."

She shrugged him off and went down the hall, closely followed by another batch of agents. They ignored her, focused on the task at hand.

The first agent knocked on the door three times before kicking it in. Claire had the absurd thought that Chip was going to hit the roof when he heard about the broken door. As if that was the greatest of their worries!

Claire stood, mouth hanging open, listening to the shouts of the agents. Within moments, she heard an "All clear!"

She crept closer, watching as agents ransacked the room. One was pulling the sheets off the bed, while two others were ripping the drawers from the dresser and dumping the contents onto the floor. One emerged from under the bed holding a brown, thin wallet.

"We've got something," he said, brushing past Claire.

Agent McCoy accepted it, and Claire watched as he opened it to reveal Marty's driver's license, smiling behind the plastic insert.

Her heart ached. *Poor Marty.*

"There it is," he said, beaming.

A license! That was all they'd found. Marty had gotten away. She knew she shouldn't say anything, but she couldn't help it. "There what is?"

That little bit of snark was hard to contain. If she was about to be arrested, she'd save her next words for the presence of her attorney.

But it ended up being worse than that. Nobody came to arrest her. No one even made a move. She stood there, dumbfounded, watching them scurrying around her. It wasn't until Lucy burst out of her room down the hall that they perked up.

"Claire!" she yelled, waving.

Agent McCoy took a step forward. "Lucy? Lucy Woodley?"

She ran over, eyes wild. "Yes. Please, don't –"

He grabbed one of her wrists and swung it behind her back. "You are under arrest for concealing a fugitive."

"What?" Lucy shot him an offended look as he clipped the first handcuff on.

Claire wanted to scream. "No, you don't understand –"

The agent's face brightened. "Would you like to confess to the crime instead, then?"

"Don't worry, Claire," Lucy said breezily. "This isn't my first rodeo."

Claire had no idea what that meant until she remembered Lucy being arrested for protesting a few years prior.

This was different, though. Claire tried to follow, but someone held her back. She turned around to see the somber face of Agent Alvarez. "I'm sorry about this, Claire," he said.

She shook her head. "You don't understand, this isn't – we're not some crime family!"

He let out a sigh. "If you have an attorney, now is the time to call them."

What a nightmare.

But he was right. She rushed back to her room and made a call to the best defense attorney that she knew in Seattle: Melanie Black. Claire had worked under her when she was a public defender. She was bold, fierce and fought for her clients like an angry momma bear – just the way Claire felt now.

Claire's call was answered, and when she said it was an emergency, she was put through to Melanie's cell phone. She left an urgent voicemail explaining that her daughter had been arrested.

Luckily, Melanie returned her call in record time, listened to Claire's hurried version of events, and told her that she'd meet her at the federal detention center in Seattle in two hours.

As soon as they got off the phone, Claire pulled up the ferry schedule to see how quickly she could get to the mainland. To her disappointment, the next ferry didn't leave for an hour and a half.

She called the only person she could think of: Margie.

"I'll call Hank right away," Margie said. "He can get us to the mainland and we'll rent a car from there, okay?"

Claire nodded. "Okay."

"It's going to be fine, Claire. You'll see. I'll be with you every step of the way."

Claire swallowed. Her throat felt so dry. "I don't know, Margie. I never should have come here. I never should have bought this hotel, I –"

"Oh no you don't! There won't be any pity parties while I'm with you. I'll be over in half an hour. Go and pack a bag. Do you hear me?"

"Yes," Claire said with a sigh.

She hung up the phone, dumping the contents of her overnight bag to make room for Lucy's things. Would Lucy even be allowed to have anything?

She wasn't sure, but she was going to bring as much as she could. Claire was on her way to Lucy's room when her phone rang.

Chip.

Her stomach sank. Everything he'd said to her was true. It was her fault that the FBI had descended onto the hotel, and if the hotel didn't make it another year, that too was entirely her fault. He was right, and the shame burned deep in her soul.

She almost didn't answer his call, but it seemed worse to ignore him. "Hi," she said weakly.

"Claire, are you okay?" he asked.

She sighed. "I'm sorry, Chip. Now isn't a good time."

"I heard." He paused. "Uh, would you mind stopping by my house for a minute? It's not far."

Did he want to yell at her in person? "I can't. I need to get to Seattle. I'm sorry – about everything. It's my fault. I know it is. You were right." She paused. "I've never been more sorry in all of my life."

She ended the call and turned her phone off. That was enough. Perhaps they'd never speak again. It'd be for the best.

Chapter Twenty-seven

Chip tried calling Claire again, but his call went to voicemail.

"No luck?" asked Marty.

Chip shook his head. "Do you have any proof that this program is dangerous?"

"Of course not," Marty said. "That's why they locked me out of it."

Chip nodded and grabbed his jacket. "All right, you stay here. When the phone rings, answer it. You got me?"

"Where are you going?" asked Marty, standing up to follow him.

"To get you an audience with an old friend. Be ready to talk about that program."

Marty nodded and waved him off.

Chip got into his truck and drove to the small airport on the island. He didn't fly often these days, but the staff all knew him.

"Hey Chip!" said Mara, the lone employee, when she saw him walk in. "How's it going?"

He leaned on the counter. "Not bad. How are you doing?"

"Can't complain," she said with a sigh. "What's up?"

"I need to catch a flight to the mainland."

She nodded. "Where are you headed?"

"New York City, but I don't know how yet."

"Hm." She clicked through her computer screen. "I don't have anything. You need it today?"

He nodded. "As soon as possible."

"I still owe you one for getting my parents that room in the hotel last Christmas..." Mara paused before breaking into a smile. "If you're feeling adventurous, I think I have something for you."

"Oh yeah?"

She tapped a finger on the counter. "How urgent is this trip?"

"Extremely."

She leaned forward. "All right, we have a private jet flying out in forty minutes. I can sneak you onto it."

Chip raised his eyebrows. "You mean in the wheel well?"

"No," Mara said with a laugh. "I'll tell them you're a mechanic, that you'll be working on the plane in the hangar in New York."

Incredible. "That would be amazing."

She smiled, leaning down and pulling a small tool bag from under the counter. "I'll tell the pilot, Rick. He won't say a word. Just don't talk too much and try to look handy, okay?"

He nodded, accepting the bag. "Thanks Mara. I owe you one, now."

"Nah." She shook her head. "We're even."

When the paying customer arrived for his flight, Chip was already on board and in the cockpit. Rick said hello, and the man in the business suit nodded as he walked by.

"Nice to meet you," he said before taking a seat and opening his laptop.

Not much need for lying, even. The guy didn't care.

In the cockpit, Rick and Chip got along fine. Though Rick had a habit of rambling about everything from conspiracies about the fabric softener industry to complaints about men's hair coloring products, he didn't ask many questions. Chip was thankful for that, and happy to be able to feign listening as he worked through ideas in his head.

They reached New York City in a matter of hours, landing at the small, private Teterboro Airport. Their passenger, whose name Chip never learned, deplaned promptly before disappearing into a waiting black car.

Chip was able to drop his ruse, leaving the tool bag on board for the return flight.

"Are you heading back to Orcas Island today?" asked Chip.

Rick nodded. "I expect so, in a few hours. I'll just be waiting here until he gets back."

No wonder this guy had so much time to think up conspiracies. "A few hours. All right."

"I'm happy to fly you back."

"Thanks Rick. I hope I can make it."

Chip caught a cab into Manhattan. It was a short half-hour drive, but it felt much longer. His mind was racing. Though he'd had the entire flight to figure out what to say, he was still unsure exactly how, or if, his plan would work.

When the cab dropped him off in town, his first stop was to a clothing store. He hadn't thought to change before leaving, and no one would find his thick fisherman's sweater charming here.

He moved quickly, picking up a black T-shirt and a gray sport coat. When he'd worked on Wall Street, he'd worn a suit every day. This was a cooler, younger look – more of a Silicon Valley type thing. He was a bit old for it, sure, but he figured he could pull it off with some confidence.

Chip got to the building and encountered his first challenge: security. The woman working behind the desk looked bright and attentive. He decided it wasn't in his best interest to lie to her.

"Hey there. I'm Chip Douglas, and I worked with Steel Montgomery ten years ago. I'm here to save him from financial ruin."

The security guard laughed. "Oh, that's interesting."

Chip smiled. "I'd appreciate it if you could call up to his office and let his secretary know that I'm here."

She raised an eyebrow, but apparently was willing to humor him. She picked up the phone and dialed. "Yeah hey, I've got Chip Douglas down here." A pause. "Mhm, okay, I'll let him know. Hang on."

She set the phone down, pressing the "hold" button, and looked at Chip. "She said she'd be happy to schedule a meeting with Steel. His next opening is in seven weeks."

"Ah." He leaned in. "Could you have his secretary pass him a message for me?"

The security guard nodded, picking up the phone receiver. "Go ahead."

"Tell him he's about to get stuck on the Ferris wheel again, and there's no getting off this time."

She smiled, slightly puzzled, and repeated back his words before hanging up the phone. "You can wait here, Mr. Douglas."

"Thanks." He took a seat in the lobby, watching as people came and went – busy, full of importance, and not noticing him in the least. Chip was glad he'd bought the jacket. It felt like it was suffocating him, but it did keep him from looking like a total intruder.

The security desk phone rang nearly forty minutes later. The conversation was brief.

"Mr. Douglas?"

He stood and approached the desk. "Yes?"

She pulled out a visitor pass, scanning it into a machine. "You can go up to the eighty-second floor. Just use this."

He smiled, accepting the pass. "Thank you."

The elevator took him up without stopping, and Steel was waiting for him when the doors opened.

"Chip! My man! I thought you were dead."

Chip shook his hand. "Not yet, Steel."

"Come on in. I've got a late lunch coming up. Would you like anything? It's just lobster, but I can get whatever you like."

Chip shook his head. "No, thanks. I don't want to take much of your time."

He led them into an office absolutely stuffed with sparkling black granite. Even the desk was made of heavy stone, polished and shining.

They both sat down and Steel made a face. "Why do I feel like you're going to tell me about an exciting investment opportunity?"

"That must be your next meeting," Chip quipped.

Steel laughed. "Right. You're here to remind me about the time I almost died at the county fair."

Almost died. He was such an exaggerator. He'd gotten stuck on that Ferris wheel for forty minutes, tops. He probably could've gotten off sooner, too, if it weren't for his determination to make a deal with the guy who was stuck with him. A deal, as it turned out, that had nearly ruined him.

Chip hid his annoyance. "Remind you of it, yeah. And warn you that you're about to do it again."

"Oh no. You're the ghost of Christmas future?" Steel chuckled, getting up to pick up a bottle of dark liquor. "Would you like one?"

Chip shook his head. "No thanks."

"How's the wife?"

"Quite happy. She finally divorced me."

Steel laughed, hard, going as far as slapping his knee. "Still the same old Chip. Never change buddy."

Chip wasn't here to pretend they were still friends. "I've got some information about SureFired."

Steel's smile lingered. "Do you?"

He nodded. Steel was suspicious of him – he always was – but Chip had no reason to lie.

He cleared his throat. "After the crash, I moved out to Orcas Island. Have you ever been there?"

Steel shook his head. "Can't say that I've had the pleasure. Been too busy."

"It's an island not too far from Seattle. It doesn't get touched by wildfires, at least not yet."

"That's lucky," Steel said, taking a sip of his drink.

"We get smoke sometimes, though. Days where you can't go outside, where the sun is blocked out. If you crack the window, the air burns in your throat."

Steel let out a sigh and shook his head. "Terrible, isn't it?"

"It is, but it's the rest of the state that really gets destroyed."

"Hey man, I'm *right* there with you. I agree that we gotta do something about this. We gotta help."

Chip wasn't going to fall for that. He knew Steel. The only person Steel ever dreamt of helping was himself. "I heard about SureFired in a roundabout way, and I think it sounds great."

"Thank you."

"Which is why I'm sorry to tell you this, but it's going to ruin you." Chip let the words hang in the air for a moment.

The smile faded from Steel's face. "You know, Chip, we still talk about you sometimes."

There was a change in his posture; the teeth were coming out. "I'm not in the game anymore, Steel. Trust me."

He stood. "We talk about how you couldn't hack it. Some guys can't hack it, and that's what we tell the new recruits. That's why your name comes up. *You're* a warning, Chip. Not me."

"You're right, I couldn't hack it. I'm not trying to."

"Yet you come to my office and start making declarations about my ruin?"

He shrugged. "I had to get your attention."

Steel set his empty glass down. "I thank you for your concern, but I've got a lot going on today."

He sure did – the lobster was just rolling in on a cloth-draped cart. Steel waved the server off without looking at him.

Chip wasn't going to budge. He knew he was getting somewhere, especially with Steel's angry reaction. "They sold you a lie. The program isn't ready. It can't predict anything. Not yet. It might in a year or two, but not yet."

Steel shrugged. "That's not for you to decide."

"It hasn't been applied to a single fire season," Chip continued. "Don't you want to be fully developed before you deploy it?"

Steel sat down. "I consider myself an early adopter."

"I'm all for early adopting," Chip said, leaning forward. "The problem is that the alerts *don't work*. There are going to be headlines all across the country: Steel and Steal Causes Hundreds of Deaths."

He sat back, putting his feet up on the desk. "It's been really nice catching up with you, man. I'll have the company car sent up. They'll take you anywhere you want to go. Go back to your fire-scorched home, maybe. Is it true that ash falls from the sky?"

"They're overcharging you, too. It's not ready, they know it, and I can prove it."

Steel stiffened. "Overcharging me? How?"

"It comes down to the technology," Chip said. "It takes time to get all of these factors into the program, to test them, to make sure they're right."

"I know that," Steele said.

There it was. Bravado. "Exactly. You're a smart guy. I know that from working with you. I'm going make a call to one of the first programmers of SureFired, and you can decide for yourself."

Chip waited as Steel seemed to debate this.

"Unless you don't want to hear it," Chip added.

Steel sat back and waved a hand. "I don't care. Call him."

Chip nodded, dialing his home number and setting the phone on the table between then.

Marty answered as instructed. "Hello?"

"Marty, it's Chip. I'm here with Steel Montgomery. Have you two met before?"

"We've had phone calls twice before," Marty said.

Chip looked at Steel, who nodded. "Nice to hear from you again, Marty."

"You too, sir."

Chip suppressed smile. Smooth move on Marty's part, calling him "sir" – Steel loved that kind of stuff.

"Marty, tell him what you told me."

It was like releasing a herd of bulls into the office – facts, figures, differing values. Marty was convincing, even without his pictures, and on top of that, he managed to keep it brief.

When he stopped talking, Steel spoke. "Why wasn't I told any of this?"

"I tried, sir. When I brought up my concerns to the CEO, I was locked out of the building. Now the FBI is looking for me."

"The FBI?" Steel stood again, pacing.

There it was.

"Everything I do is above board," Steel said. "Everything. Why is the FBI involved? Is the SureFired team involved in fraud?"

"Not yet, sir. They didn't like what I had to say, so they claimed I was selling proprietary information to China."

Steel rolled his eyes. "Even the Chinese wouldn't pay as much for this company as I'm paying."

"SureFired needed to get ahead of this," Chip said. "They needed to leave you holding the bag."

Steel crossed his arms and faced Chip. "How do I know that you're not trying to buy the company out from under me?"

Chip laughed, loudly. "I'm broke, Steel. I work at a hotel. I have no interest in buying the company. I just don't want to see that headline about the little girl who didn't make it out in time – because her parents trusted SureFired."

Steel cringed. "What a nightmare."

"Yeah."

He leaned down to talk at the cell phone. "Marty, is there anyone I can talk to who can confirm this?"

"And clear your name?" added Chip.

There was a pause before Marty spoke. "I think so, yes. Talk to Courtney Holmes – she's the CEO's secretary. She can't afford to lose her job, but if you promise to protect her, she might tell you everything. She has access to all of the emails, the meetings – everything."

Steel's face lit up. Chip knew it was only because he could see the dollar signs, the discount he was about to get, but it didn't matter. He was on the case.

"Thanks for seeing me, Steel." Chip stood, shaking his hand. "I should be getting back."

"Hey, I'll have to visit you sometime," Steel said brightly, his mood again buoyant.

"Yeah," Chip replied. He knew it would never happen. If all went well, he'd never have to see Steel Montgomery again. "I'd be happy to host you...on a non-smoky day."

Steel laughed, patting him on the shoulder. "Same old Chip."

Chapter Twenty-eight

The boat coasted toward The Grand Madrona Hotel's dock and Claire stood, watching. It seemed like Hank wasn't in any special hurry when he pulled up. He smiled and waved, the sun illuminating his face.

"Hop in!" yelled Margie. "It's a little bumpy out there, but Hank thinks we'll make it just fine."

Claire forced a smile and stepped onto the boat with a hand from Hank.

"Now," he said, crossing his arms. "Do either of you ladies want to tell me what's going on?"

Margie tightened her scarf. "Why would you think something's going on?"

"Well," he said slowly, "your voice keeps getting shaky and I caught you staring off into the horizon with a glassy look in your eyes."

Margie frowned. "I did not get a glassy look in my eyes!"

"It's okay, Margie," said Claire. "You can tell him."

"Tell him what?" she asked innocently.

Claire took a seat. The choppiness of the water was making her feel ill. "I'm sure you'll hear all about it soon, Hank. Lucy was just arrested by the FBI."

"That's a doozy," he said casually. "FBI, huh?"

She nodded. "Yep."

He looked down at her. "Does this have anything to do with that guy they've been looking for?"

Claire nodded. "It does."

"That's quite enough!" said Margie, pushing buttons until the boat's engine started. "Hank, if you ask anything else then you're going to be involved. I know you don't like getting involved."

He waved a hand, taking over the steering wheel. "I'm not going to ask any more questions. I'm sure I'll find out soon enough."

Claire smiled. He seemed unworried by it all – so different from Margie. "Are you going to turn me in, Hank?"

"I can't turn you in if you haven't done anything – that I know about," he said, throwing the boat into reverse and slowly exiting the harbor. "The truth is, if anything has happened, I know my beautiful wife probably had a hand in it."

"Excuse me, Mr. Kowalski," Margie said, hands on her hips. "Why would you assume it's my fault?"

He laughed. "I didn't say it was your fault. Just that you might've had a hand in it. There's nothing that happens on these islands that you don't know about – usually long before I do."

She considered this for a moment and let out a little laugh. "Maybe people tell me things because I'm such a good listener."

He beamed. "That must be it."

Claire stared at them, watching this exchange. There was once a time when she thought she could do the same thing that Margie had done – that she could move to the islands, start a new business, and forge a new place in the world.

She'd never admit this to anyone, but she'd also hoped she'd get the chance to fall in love, too. It seemed silly, even immature to hope that. Her love life had always been disappointing in one way or another. There was no reason it would change because she moved.

Claire thought there might have been something between her and Chip, that they understood each other, that they had something...unique.

That, too, was silly.

As it turned out, Claire was the opposite of Margie. Instead of inspiring confidence and joy, Claire brought ruin to all. Instead of falling in love with a charming guy, she drove him away.

Claire sunk into her seat and focused on fighting the nausea.

They sailed on, Margie filling the conversation with stories about recent clients she'd had at Saltwater Cove. Hank added some details Margie left out, and Claire sat silently, listening.

When they reached Anacortes, Hank gave Margie a kiss and told her to be careful.

"I'm always careful," she said.

He smiled. "Right. Claire, keep an eye on her. Let me know if you need a ride back. I'll be waiting for your call."

Margie smiled at him and squeezed his hand. "Thanks sweetie."

Waiting on her call. Claire had never had a guy wait on her call. More pathetically, she'd always waited on theirs. Perhaps romance wasn't meant for everyone. It certainly wasn't meant for her.

They took a taxi from the dock to the car rental office. Margie had already arranged for a car, and it was waiting for them when they arrived.

"Do you want me to drive?" Margie asked. "I'm sure you're still quite shaken up."

Claire nodded. "That would be nice."

They started their drive to Seattle and Claire didn't know what to say. She couldn't get over what a wonderful friend Margie was, and how guilty she felt about the whole affair. She hoped this favor wouldn't land Margie in trouble too.

Margie wouldn't let the silence stand, of course, and after twenty minutes she made her first demand. "All right, Claire," she said, looking over. "Spill it."

"Spill what?"

Margie let out a sigh, turning down the radio. "Tell me what happened."

"I'm still not quite sure." Claire paused. "The FBI searched the room where Marty was staying and found his wallet."

"Oh no! Did they find him, too?"

"No," Claire said. "I don't think so."

"Do you know where he is?"

Claire shook her head. "I don't. I feel awful. I promised that I would keep him safe and…"

"He is safe, Claire. I'm sure of it."

Claire wasn't so sure. She sat in silence.

Margie spoke again. "Why is Lucy in trouble?"

"They said that she'd concealed a fugitive. I guess because the room was in her name? I never should have let her do that. I should've kept him at the cabin."

"What's done is done," Margie said matter-of-factly. "From here, there's nothing left to do but to figure it out together."

Claire said nothing. It would be best if she weren't involved in the figuring out. She had done quite enough already.

Melanie met them outside of the prison. "I had a chance to speak to Lucy. She's doing well."

"Is she?" Claire asked. Her heart felt broken.

Melanie gave her a reassuring smile. "Of course. They're not mistreating her, and she isn't afraid. In fact, she's being rather sassy with them."

Margie chuckled. "I bet she is."

Claire felt like she was going to be sick again. "Is it a serious charge?"

"It is." Melanie frowned. "They're not really after her, though. They're after Marty."

Claire narrowed her eyes. "What does that mean?"

"It means don't say anything about him out here that you don't want them to know," Melanie said in a low voice.

"They're offering to drop the charges if Lucy will tell them where he is."

Claire nodded. "I see."

"Did she tell them?" asked Margie.

Melanie shook her head. "No, she's refusing to say anything. I told her we can work out a deal, keep her record clean. She's protective of this guy, though. Do you know who he is, Claire?"

Claire nodded. "I do."

"Can you get her to talk?"

She let out a sigh. "I don't think anyone can get Lucy to do something she doesn't want to do."

"No, that ship has surely sailed," Margie added.

"This is all my fault," Claire groaned. "What will happen if she's convicted?"

"That's a big if," Melanie said. "Don't forget, they don't have much evidence on her. I have hopes that I could sway a jury."

"But if not?"

"If not, it's up to a five-year sentence," Melanie said.

It felt like the earth shifted beneath her. Claire took a seat on a nearby bench. "Five *years*."

"Don't fret, not yet," Melanie said. "I need to go back in, but maybe you can visit later today?"

Claire nodded. "Thanks, Mel."

She smiled, squeezing Claire's shoulder before returning inside.

Margie waited a moment before speaking again. "How are you doing?"

Claire shook her head. "This is all my fault."

"It is not your fault!" Margie promptly said. "I thought I told you no pity parties today."

"But it is my fault, Margie. What was I thinking? That I could handle this all on my own? I'm a failure. An utter failure."

Margie crossed her arms. "You don't really believe all of that, do you?"

Claire bowed her head for a moment, and the dizziness hit her again. "Yes, I do. It's just – it's even worse than I could've imagined."

"Why are you beating yourself up like this?"

"Because, Margie." Claire looked up at her. "The one thing that I have been good at in my life is being a mom. I never had a great career, I never dressed well or had interesting things to say at parties. I can't garden. I'm a terrible baker –"

"That's not true," Margie countered. "You make excellent cookies. And lemon bars."

Claire smiled. "It's just that after the girls got through school and started moving on with their lives, I felt so...empty. I felt like I'd lost my purpose. They didn't need me anymore."

"Of course they need you. They'll always need you."

"Yes, but it's different." Claire shifted. This bench was freezing. "I spent so much time and energy raising them to be strong and independent women. Now that they are strong and independent women, I don't know what to do with myself."

Margie laughed and took a seat next to her. "Now you have to learn how to be a mom to strong, independent women. That's a change for you, too."

"I just don't feel like..." Claire's voice trailed off. She wasn't sure how to put it into words. She'd had this odd feeling for years now.

It crept in on her when she was alone, especially when she was people-watching. It was like she didn't fit, she didn't belong. She thought moving would change that, but it only made her feel worse.

"Like what?" asked Margie, grabbing her hand.

Claire debated if she should say any more, but there was no use in burying it. Hiding how she felt hadn't helped, either. "I feel like I don't belong anywhere in this world. Like I can't find my place."

Margie squeezed her hand. "Oh, Claire. A lot of people feel that way. I felt that way! It's hard to find your footing when the world keeps on changing."

"You've done so well though, Margie. You met Hank and started your business. I ran off, bought a hotel that I don't know the first thing about, then found out about a new family member," she dropped her voice, "and promptly ruined his life and Lucy's."

Margie wrapped an arm around Claire's shoulder. "Come here, my sweet friend. You haven't ruined anyone's life. You're a wonderful mother. You always were, and you always will be. I'm sure that Mar – I mean, your new family member – appreciates everything that you've done."

"What have I done?" Claire shook her head, tears shaking in her eyes. "What have I done for anyone but make things worse?"

"You've loved them – really loved them. That means more than you know."

Claire sniffled. She wished she had some tissues, and as if by magic, Margie pulled two from her purse.

"Why do you think that new family member chose to stick around?"

Claire shrugged. "Desperation?"

"No," Margie said with a chuckle. "Love. And look at Lucy!"

"Poor Lucy..." Claire said, her voice breaking.

"Not poor Lucy! How many people could withstand questioning and stick to their morals? You should be proud."

Claire nodded. "I am proud, but..."

"A little FBI raid isn't going to ruin the hotel. Who told you that? You've put so much care and effort into that place already. It's going to be fabulous. You took a risk, that's all. Risks never pay off right away. Usually it's painful to begin with, then rocky all the way through."

Claire let out a sigh. She could breathe out of her nose again, which was a small victory. "You're right, but –"

"Not 'but!' That's how it is. If it were easy, everyone would do it. Don't worry about the hotel. I'm sure that handsome Chip can help you."

Claire grimaced. "Chip will never forgive me."

"I wouldn't be so sure." Margie said. "I saw the way he looked at you."

"Margie," Claire shot her a look. "You say that about everyone. Just because you love me doesn't mean that everyone does."

"I'm right this time. I know it." Margie stood. "Okay, before you go to see Lucy, I'm going to get you a nice, hot cup of tea and something to eat. I'm ashamed to say I didn't have anything homemade to bring along on short notice."

Claire laughed. Leave it to Margie to be disappointed for not having a lunch packed into her purse. "That's all right. I'm fine."

"This is not a negotiation," Margie said, shaking her head. "You can either stay here or tag along. It'll only take a few minutes."

Claire smiled. "I'll wait it out. Thanks, Margie."

After half a cup of tea and a scone, Claire got the call to come see Lucy. The visitation was like something out of a movie, with Lucy behind a plate of glass, in a prisoner fish tank.

The only comfort was that Lucy didn't seem distressed. Her hair even looked nice.

Claire wished she could give her a long hug. She had to settle with talking to her through the black wall phone. "Hi sweetheart. I've been so worried for you."

Lucy snickered. "Oh, don't be. I've been in *far* worse prisons than this. This place is nice! It looks like my old dorm room."

"How many prisons have you been in?" Claire asked, alarmed.

She let out a sigh. "I guess they were technically jails? When they were going to bulldoze that historic library in Oregon, I probably got arrested three times for that alone."

Claire shook her head. "You're something else, Lucy."

"The library is still standing, and so am I."

Claire leaned in. "Melanie told me about the deal they offered."

Lucy rolled her eyes. "I have no idea where the fugitive is, and if I did, I wouldn't tell them anyway."

Claire couldn't help but smile. "I see."

The guard announced that visitation would be over in one minute.

"Is there anything that I can get you?" asked Claire.

Lucy shook her head. "Don't worry about me. Really. I'm fine."

"I'll be staying at a hotel nearby, and I'm coming to visit first thing in the morning. I love you, honey."

Lucy smiled. "I love you too, Mom."

The tears caught in Claire's throat. Lucy never called her "Mom" except when she was feeling especially mushy. Claire rushed out of the area and burst into tears once she was safely out of sight.

Margie stayed with her at the hotel that night, reading aloud from websites about felony charges, how long the sentence could be, and options like house arrest and community service.

Claire didn't find it all that comforting, but she was glad, at least, that Lucy wasn't being mistreated. There was a small part of her that felt obligated to call in to the hotel and check on things, but she didn't have the strength. She fell asleep after setting an alarm for six the next morning.

When her alarm went off, she leapt out of bed and took a quick shower. As she and Margie were getting ready, Margie announced that she had a text from Hank. "He says he knows what we were up to, and he's going to arrest us when we get back."

Claire's stomach dropped. "Why?"

"He's just kidding," Margie said with a laugh. "Oh, here's another text. He's a slow typer, you know. He says, 'Joking, the FBI sent out a notice that there is no longer a person of interest on the islands.'"

"What does that mean?" Claire asked. "Do you think they caught Marty?"

"No, I wouldn't say that." Margie shook her head. "That would be news – the biggest news the islands have seen all year."

That calmed her a bit. "That's true."

"Let's see if the prison can tell us anything," suggested Margie.

Claire agreed and they headed out to the car. On their way, Claire got a call from Melanie.

"I've got some great news! They decided to drop the charges. You can pick Lucy up today."

"What?" Claire felt like her heart would burst. "Does that mean that she –"

"Nope. They have no interest in Marty anymore. It looks like some new evidence came to light. I think he may be off the hook too, but I'm not sure yet."

Her heart thundered in her chest. "This is incredible."

Melanie laughed. "Easiest case of the year. If he does need help, though, give me a call. It was so nice seeing you, Claire. I've missed working with you!"

That was when she used to be good at her job...but Claire was too excited to let that melancholy thought drift in. "Oh, Melanie, I can't tell you how much your help meant to me. I've missed you too. Promise you'll come up and visit the hotel!"

"I was hoping you'd invite me!" Melanie said with a laugh.

Claire smiled. "Any time, really."

Once Claire hung up the phone, Margie turned to her. "See? It's all working out!"

"I don't understand how. Is this a trick?"

Margie shook her head. "Melanie wouldn't trick you. The tides are turning, my friend!"

When they arrived at the prison, Agents Alvarez and McCoy were waiting for them.

Agent Alvarez greeted her with a smile and a handshake. "Miss Cooke, so nice to see you again. I was just about to go and help Lucy find her way out."

"Thank you," she said, beaming.

When he walked off, Agent McCoy took a step forward. "I've got some good news and some bad news."

Claire felt her muscles tighten. "What's the good news?"

"We've received evidence that shows Marty is innocent. We're done looking for him."

"You're kidding!" she said. "Wait. Are you kidding?"

He laughed and shook his head. "No, I'm not."

"Yay!" Margie clapped her hands together.

"What's the bad news?" asked Claire.

"The bad news is that I behaved like – er, I mean, I was wrong." He let out a heavy sigh. "I was harsh with you, and I'm sorry for that. I hope you'll consider my apology."

Claire smiled. "No apology needed. You were doing your job."

"But maybe you should work on your listening skills," added Margie.

They laughed, and a moment later, Lucy emerged from behind a heavy metal door, a broad smile on her face.

Chapter Twenty-nine

Instead of rushing back to the airport, Chip decided he should make the most of his time in New York. His son James had moved back to the city after finishing his journalism degree. Chip always missed him, but seeing Marty, who was so close to James' age, made it worse.

Like many young people, James was usually busy and impossible to pin down, but he answered his phone on the second ring. "Daddio! How's it going?"

"Hey James! I'm doing pretty well. How about you?"

"Same."

"I know this is short notice," Chip continued, "but I'm in town and thought we could meet up. Dinner, maybe?"

"You know I never say no to a free dinner."

Chip laughed. "Mom doesn't let you into her kitchen anymore?"

"She does, but I'm getting old, so that's starting to get embarrassing."

"But you're not embarrassed to get a free meal from me?"

James' answer was instant. "Nope."

They met for dinner at a restaurant of James' choice: a small, Korean joint with space for only four tables. The employees recognized James and immediately started joking with him. It made Chip happy and sad at the same time. Happy that James had built a life for himself here, and sad that it was so far from Orcas.

Chip didn't even have to bring it up. James admitted he was overdue for a visit. "Work's just been so busy."

Chip nodded. "You're still enjoying it, though?"

"Oh yeah, it's been great. I mean, I'm putting in long hours, but I feel like I'm getting ahead."

"That's good." Chip smiled. James reminded him of himself at that age, though he'd chosen a far less noble career.

James was different than Chip in some important ways. He had a lot that he cared about. His job was as an investigative reporter, chasing stories about corruption and greed. He had a strong moral fiber, which he must've gotten from his mother. Young Chip had only cared about getting rich.

"Are things okay at the hotel?" asked James.

"Yeah, I think so. We had a little run-in with the FBI recently, but that might sort itself out."

James raised his eyebrows. "Are you telling me this because you're on your way out of the country?"

"No," Chip said, laughing. "Not this time. The FBI showed up partially because of a guest – and partially because of our new owner."

"Oh right! How's he doing?"

Chip took a sip of his soda. "She's doing great. I was a bit hard on her at the start, but to tell you the truth, she's incredible."

"Wow, high praise from you." James took a bite of his meal. "What brought you all the way out here, then?"

Chip let out a sigh. "If I told you, I'd have to –"

"Don't finish that," said James, laughing. "I'm just joking. I'm always interested in a good story. What happened?"

Chip sat back. "I'm not sure where to start, honestly. There are still some legal issues unresolved, but if they get resolved, I'll tell you all about it."

James shot him a concerned look. "Again, not your legal issues, right?"

"No, no." Chip waved a hand. "Thankfully not. For once, I did the right thing. I think you'll be proud of me."

James smiled. "I'm always proud of you, Dad."

James had to get back to work not long after that, but he promised that he'd come and visit soon. Chip wished him luck and told him he was welcome any time.

So much time had passed that Chip was certain flying with Rick was no longer an option. It was worth it to spend time with James. He pulled out his phone and booked the next, very expensive, flight back to Seattle.

It was a red-eye, and when he got in, there were no ferries for several hours. He decided to get a hotel room and catch some sleep before booking the express ferry to Friday Harbor, then the interisland ferry to Orcas.

As he stood on the deck of the ferry to Orcas Island, he could barely keep his eyes open. Even though it was beautiful, he was so tired. No wonder no one ever wanted to visit him. The trip took too long.

But as soon as he saw that beautiful island in the distance, he felt full of life again. The crystal-clear water, the miles and miles of trees and towering mountains – there was no other place like it on earth.

He landed at the ferry terminal and managed to convince Rhonda to pick him up.

"Where have you been?" Rhonda said as she popped open her passenger door. "We got raided yesterday!"

"I know, I know. I was trying to handle it." He took a seat, shutting the door.

She pointed at him to buckle his seat belt. "You have no idea. They made a huge mess, and then they just left."

Chip laughed. "I'm sorry. It won't happen again."

"It had better not," she said. "Or I will call the FBI myself and demand they send a second super special team to clean up their mess."

She dropped him off at home, and Chip was disappointed to find that Marty had disappeared without a trace. The poor kid was probably traumatized from being hunted. Hopefully he hadn't gone far, and Steel's determination to save money would prove his innocence.

When Chip got back to the hotel, he put in a call to Claire. It went to voicemail. He had the vague worry that she might've blocked his number. He was sitting at his desk, ruminating on this, when his phone rang.

"Hey Bossman."

He let out a sigh. "Hi Gigi."

"The photographers are here."

Chip thought she sounded entirely too cheerful. "Is everything okay?"

"Oh yes. You know what? I'd be happy to show them around."

That was suspicious. Chip got up from his desk and went to the lobby to investigate.

He introduced himself to Morgan, the photographer that Margie knew, and quickly realized the problem. Morgan's business partner Luke, who was apparently also her boyfriend, had caught Gigi's eye.

"You must be *so* artistic," Gigi cooed, looking up at him, doe-eyed.

"I don't know if I can claim that," he said. "That credit belongs to my better half."

Gigi shot Morgan a chilly look before returning her attention to Luke. "I love your accent. Where are you from?"

"Just outside of London. Where are you from?"

Chip suppressed a smile. He so badly wanted to tease Gigi, but didn't want to upset his new photographer. He turned to look at Morgan, however, and saw that she was ignoring this exchange entirely.

"Margie told me so many things about you and the hotel. It's just magnificent!" Morgan said.

"Thank you. That's very kind." Chip smiled. "Margie is very kind, actually."

"She is. She's the best," Morgan said with a smile.

In the background, Gigi was still droning on. "I'm more than happy to show you around, and hey, maybe you could take my picture later?"

Without addressing Gigi, Morgan unceremoniously grabbed Luke by the arm and pulled him toward her. "Chip, would you mind giving us a tour and an idea of what you'd like to get from these pictures?"

"Of course."

Much to Gigi's disappointment, they left and made a round of the hotel. Spending a few hours with them was a pleasant way to pass the time, and from the samples that Morgan showed him, Chip was impressed already. How had he missed the fact that the hotel pictures were so terrible for so long?

After they left, Chip returned to his office and resumed his wait for Claire. He finally decided to leave a message, telling her that he was at the hotel, all was well, and that he was waiting on her call.

Following that, he was glued to his phone. There was only a single ten-minute block where he was unable to answer his cell phone, and naturally, she called during that time.

Her voice sounded distressed. "Chip, I just wanted to let you know that I'm heading back to Orcas Island. I'm planning to pack up my things and, uh, get out of your hair. I'm sorry about everything that happened. I can explain, if you're willing to hear it. Lucy was released, so that's good and...well, I can tell you later. See you."

Chip could tell that she had no intention of seeing him again, but he was not going to let her walk out of his life that easily.

Chapter Thirty

The ride back to Anacortes was a breeze. Margie was still at the wheel, chatting away, but now she had Lucy to contend with, too.

"The guard said that I was the most annoying prisoner he had all week," Lucy said. "But he also said I was the funniest prisoner he'd had all week, so I'll take that as a win."

Margie nodded. "Always take the compliment."

Lucy leaned forward, perching her head between them from the backseat. "The funniest thing was when Agent McCoy tried to play bad cop with me."

"Oh yes," Claire said. "He was always bad cop to me, too."

"He never listened to a word I said," complained Lucy, "so I started telling him that he had beautiful eyes."

That made Claire laugh. "Lucy!"

"What?" She put her hands up. "It's true! There wasn't anything else true that I could tell him."

"Did you know that he apologized to me?" Claire asked, turning around to look at her. "Right before we picked you up."

Lucy sat back, her mouth open and arms crossed. "What about me? I'm the one he arrested!"

Claire laughed. "Maybe he meant to get to you next."

"Or maybe he was afraid his apology would be taken as an invitation to hit on him more," Margie said with a giggle.

Lucy shook her head. "Unbelievable. I wasn't hitting on him. He was way too old for me, and he always had coffee breath."

Claire laughed. "I'm just thankful you're out of there, and that you're okay."

"I wasn't really that worried," said Lucy. "Like Melanie said, their evidence was all circumstantial. They hoped I would be scared enough to talk about Marty."

"You still haven't heard from him?" asked Margie.

Claire shook her head, instinctively checking her phone. "Unfortunately, no. I don't know where he is or how to contact him. He's probably still on the run, poor soul."

"I checked the FBI's Most Wanted List," said Lucy. "He's not on there anymore."

"Hopefully he's still on the island," Claire said. "I'm excited to tell him the good news."

"After you find him, will you be returning to the hotel?" asked Margie.

Claire bit her lip. "I've made a decision about the hotel."

"Oh?" Lucy leaned forward again.

Claire cleared her throat. "I'm not looking for any advice. I am just letting you both know that I will be stepping away from the hotel and selling it. That's final."

Margie shot her a worried look. "Isn't that a bit rash?"

"Everything recently has been rash," replied Claire. "But not this. Buying the hotel was a mistake. I'm just going to undo it."

She then insisted on changing the topic to Lucy's job hunt, only to find out that Lucy had lied about the interview in Seattle. This occupied their conversation for the rest of the drive.

When they got to Anacortes, they returned the rental car and Hank picked them up in his boat. He dropped Lucy and Claire off on the west side of the island, and they took a taxi back to the cabin.

Claire was hoping that she'd walk through the doors and find Marty hiding inside, but she had no such luck.

Instead, it took him nearly fifteen minutes, watching from the trees in the distance, before he made himself known. He appeared in the doorway, smiling brightly.

Claire pulled him in for a tight hug. "I was afraid you'd run off for good."

"I couldn't," he said. "It's pretty hard to sneak off of an island when everyone is looking for you."

"Your own personal Alcatraz," Lucy added.

Claire filled him in on the recent happenings, and Marty couldn't believe what he was hearing. He rushed to set up his laptop, connecting to the internet to check his email.

"I'm going to disguise my IP address," he said. "In case the FBI is still watching me."

Claire didn't think they were, but she appreciated how careful he was.

He found an email from Courtney, the secretary from SureFired.

"What does it say?" asked Lucy.

Marty's eyes darted back and forth like lightning. "It's true. It's all over. They know I'm innocent! Courtney proved it!"

Lucy squealed, clapping her hands together, and Claire had the urge to do the same.

Marty continued. "The venture capital firm got insider information that the CEO was intent on defrauding them, and that they had lied about me selling the technology to cover it up. They provided all of this to the FBI, who cleared my name, and the sale price of SureFired fell by a few hundred million dollars. It's already all over the business news."

Lucy raised an eyebrow. "A few hundred million? How much was this thing worth?"

"A lot," said Marty. "Courtney said she's sorry she didn't speak up sooner, but she was afraid after seeing what happened to me."

"Anyone would be afraid after that," said Claire. "It's the reason that the CEO went after you so viciously."

Marty nodded. "I can't believe Chip managed to do it."

Claire paused. "Chip? What did he have to do with this?"

"He knew Steel Montgomery, one of the partners at Steel and Steal, the company that was going to buy SureFired. He flew to New York and got a meeting with him, then called me to explain what had happened with SureFired."

Claire had to sit down. "That's shocking."

Marty continued. "When I snuck out of the hotel before the FBI burst in, he saw me break part of the window frame and confronted me about it."

Lucy laughed. "That's hilarious. And then he decided to help you?"

"Pretty much," Marty said with a shrug. "He's sort of a scary dude, and he didn't believe me at first, but I guess he did in the end."

Lucy looked down at Claire. "Are you okay?"

She realized that she had her hand covering her mouth. "Yes, sorry. This is just a lot to take in."

Poor Chip. He'd ended up getting involved after all.

"Well, thank God for Chip," Lucy said. "Otherwise, Marty and I would've been wearing orange jumpsuits for a couple of years."

Claire shook her head. "I don't know how I'll ever repay him." Maybe by leaving the island forever...

Lucy shrugged. "You could take him on a date."

"No, Lucy," Claire said, shooting her a look before standing up to grab her coat and her purse. "I need to see him."

"Right now?" asked Lucy. "Aren't I entitled to a post-prison meal?"

Claire felt, for the first time in a week, that she knew exactly what to do. "I'll be back soon, okay?"

They didn't protest, and she rushed out of the cabin and into her car.

When she pulled up to the hotel, it looked nearly deserted. The guests must've run away in fear.

Claire pulled into a parking space and hesitated about what to do next.

What were the chances that Chip was even still there? It'd be better if she met with him in the morning, arranged a time to discuss her plan. It'd be even better if she didn't look like a prison escapee when she gave him her apology and her peace offering. She was planning to give him the hotel, no strings attached, and disappear from his life forever.

She sat, debating if it was best to wait. On the other hand, she knew he apparently hadn't hesitated to help Marty and Lucy. She wasn't going to wait, either.

Claire got out of her car and made her way to the building. As she walked through the lobby, she savored the delicate smell of lemongrass. She would miss that smell. She would miss everything about this place, especially the dream it had held for her.

A head popped up from one of the couches and surprised her. "Hey!"

She took a step back. "Chip! You're still here."

"I am." He stood. "I was hoping you'd come back tonight."

She smiled. He looked so nice, so put together. So different from how she felt. "I wasn't going to, but then I talked to Marty."

"Is he okay?"

She nodded. "He is now, thanks to you. As is Lucy. I don't know how to thank you for what you did."

"Please," he held up a hand. "It was my pleasure. I'm just glad it worked."

He was something else. "Lucy was under arrest, and I thought Marty would have nowhere to hide..." Her voice trailed off.

She closed her eyes. This wasn't how she wanted this to go. Claire started again, clearing her voice. "I'm still feeling a bit loopy, but I needed to come here and thank you in person for everything you've done."

"I'm happy I was able to help," he said gently, taking a step closer to her. "Should we talk in my office, maybe?"

She looked around. There weren't many people around, but that was a good idea. "Sure."

Claire followed him back, her eyes lingering on every beautiful detail the hotel possessed. She would miss it so much – but it was for the best.

He closed the door and they both sat down. He spoke first. "I got to see my son when I was in New York."

"How nice."

Chip nodded. "It was great to see him. He's always so busy. He asked about you, you know."

"Did he?"

"Yes. I told him that you're incredible, and I realized that I never had the guts to say that to your face."

Claire looked down. "I'm not incredible. Maybe incredibly bad for the hotel."

"No." He stared at her. "Don't say that. It's not true. You know, I got to meet Morgan today. She was wonderful, and Luke improved Gigi's day by tenfold."

"Yeah, they're great."

Chip paused before speaking again. "I've been here for years, and the whole time, I've been completely missing things. I missed the fact that our pictures were awful, and that our website made it look like the hotel was shut down, and that the bathrooms were crumbling..."

"No, you didn't –"

He continued. "I don't think I've stayed in one of these rooms once in eight years, and I put no effort into looking for improvements. The events you've planned, even the effort you put into finding Ken – "

"I know he's terrible," Claire said with a groan. "But after I hired him, I just kept hoping he would get better."

Chip laughed. "Okay, Ken was the one thing I wasn't a fan of, but even with that, you've been amazing for the hotel."

Claire let out a sigh. "Yet I still hid one of the FBI's most wanted in the hotel and put everything in danger."

"That was nothing," Chip said, waving a hand. "We've seen way worse."

She laughed. "Still. I want to apologize. It's no excuse, but I'd just found out that Marty was my nephew, and I think I had some sort of weird complex where I needed to take care of him – to prove to myself that I was still a good mother."

His face fell. "You don't have to explain yourself to me. And you're a wonderful mother. What are you talking about?"

232

"Lucy was up against five years in prison, and Marty wasn't far behind," Claire said, shaking her head. "If it weren't for you –"..."

"Maybe if you'd felt comfortable telling me any of this, we could've solved it sooner." He leaned forward. "That was my fault. From the moment I met you, I treated you like the enemy."

"You were right to," she said with a half-smile.

"No. I wasn't." He reached forward as though he was going to grab her hand, but stopped at the last second. "You made incredible changes, you have wonderful insights, and the staff loves you."

"Not Gigi."

He chuckled. "She doesn't like anyone – except Luke, and he doesn't even work here. The fact of the matter is, you're one of the best things that has ever happened to the hotel. And to me."

Claire sat back. What could he mean by that? It didn't matter. She needed to tell him what she'd decided. "I've made up my mind about the hotel."

He cocked his head to the side. "Oh?"

"I'm giving it to you. I'll step down. It'll be like I was never here."

Chip sat back and crossed his arms. "That's impossible."

She shrugged. "It's my hotel. I can sell it to whomever I want. I'll sell it to you for a dollar."

He shook his head. "No, it's impossible for me to pretend you were never here. I don't want the hotel, not like that."

She let out a sigh. "What do you want, then?"

He was quiet for a moment, his stare unbroken. "You," he finally said.

Those butterflies erupted in her chest. "Did Margie tell you to say that?"

"No." He looked down for a moment. "But she did give me the smallest of hopes that you might have feelings for me, too."

Claire cleared her throat, but she couldn't think of what to say.

He spoke again. "I'm about to make a fool of myself, so I'll make it brief."

She watched as he got up from his seat and walked over to her. She didn't protest when he took her hand in his. His hand was so warm, so comforting.

Chip let out a sigh. "I felt something, working with you for these past weeks. I felt it so strongly that sometimes I didn't know how to behave."

Claire giggled and squeezed his hand. "You behaved just fine."

"I can't imagine staying here without you. I don't want the hotel. I want you, Claire. I want every bit of you, and if you leave, I'll have no choice but to follow."

She couldn't believe what she was hearing. "I thought I was imagining things."

He shook his head, inching closer. "No."

Her heart was singing. She couldn't bear it any longer. "I guess, for your sake, I'll stay."

His smile reached his eyes. "You will?"

She nodded, and in the next second his lips were on hers, pulling her in. She threw her arms around his neck as her spirit soared, flying past all that she had ever dreamed and beyond.

Epilogue

It wasn't until March that Marty got to meet his other cousins, Lillian and Rose. They came to Orcas Island to see the hotel and to finally hear the truth about Claire's inheritance.

They were shocked by Claire's news, but they both handled it well. Lucy had already told them all about Marty's FBI escapades, so there wasn't much for him to explain there, which was nice.

The visit was short, but they made the time to commemorate the twenty-ninth anniversary of the plane crash, as well as Claire's birthday. The twins also got Marty a gift – a shirt that read "FBI's Most Wanted."

He tried to act annoyed when he opened it, but it was too hard. The girls were giggling like fools. Marty ended up holding it up to his chest and telling them dryly, "Thanks. I'll cherish this forever."

They weren't able to visit for very long, but they both promised to return soon. Marty sincerely hoped they would. He wanted to get to know them better.

Lucy cleared off not long after that, taking a new job in Seattle. "It's about time I had an income again," she reasoned. "Besides, maybe this job will be The One?"

Marty sorely missed her after she left. He'd never had a sibling growing up, but he'd always wanted one. As a kid, he'd imagined having a little brother, of course, but Lucy was like the big sister he never knew he needed.

Marty had decisions to make, too. The CEO of SureFired had been named in a lawsuit by Steel and Steal, then fired by the board.

A new CEO, Blaise Krentz, was brought in to clean things up. He reinstated Marty to his old position with a raise, and even offered to let him work remotely.

It was too good of a deal to turn down. Marty still believed in SureFired, and he wanted to see the program through. He accepted the offer, and when he swung by the office to pick up his things, his coworkers had a little welcome back party set up.

Everyone had fun with it and people apologized for doubting him. Well, everyone except for David, who never apologized for a thing, including ratting out Lucy.

It was just as well that he didn't apologize. Marty would never forgive him anyway.

With his new remote position, Marty decided to stay on Orcas Island for a while and help Claire and Chip with the hotel. He revamped the website, uploaded new pictures, and taught Chip how to run promotions online.

On top of that, he designed a program that analyzed room rates of nearby hotels. It worked constantly to suggest rate changes and predict times of lower occupancy. The program was easy for Marty to make, and ended up being a huge tool for Chip and Claire.

Not that they needed a ton of tools to run the hotel. Together, Chip and Claire were an unstoppable team. They spent all of their time together, talking about the hotel, dreaming up new promotions, working on improvements, and generally being overwhelmingly perfect together.

Marty was happy for them. It seemed like Claire had really induced a change in Chip. He was much friendlier, and he hardly scared Marty at all anymore.

Heck, he even made Marty feel like part of The Grand Madrona Team. Marty felt like he belonged, and he was starting to process the anger and hurt he'd sustained from the shock of finding out about his adoption.

After he was cleared by the FBI, he'd called his parents and had a long conversation about what had happened. His mom was horrified that she hadn't known. She said they would've flown back at once. Marty knew that was true, which was probably why he didn't tell them anything. He had been too upset with them then.

Now, though, he could acknowledge the fact that his parents loved him, even if they'd made a mistake in withholding his adoption. Marty was learning to accept that they were human, too. They couldn't wait to visit him on Orcas, though he told them to wait until the weather was better so they could enjoy the sites.

He'd been a bit worried that his mom might be jealous of Claire, too. That worry was unfounded. His mom couldn't wait to meet her. She started calling her every few weeks just to chat.

It made Marty feel happy. There was something wonderful about piecing his life back together and getting a bonus family.

Everything seemed to be getting better. By the time their first event rolled around for Easter, the hotel was running at full capacity every weekend and near eighty percent capacity during the week. Chip said it was the best he'd seen it in years.

Marty was excited for the festivities – the Easter egg hunt, the train they'd set up for the kids, and the egg painting in the lobby. As an added bonus, Lucy made a surprise visit and volunteered to don the Easter bunny suit.

She was struggling with getting the bunny head on when Marty interrupted to tell her about David's continued cold demeanor.

Lucy didn't hold back. "If that weasel *ever* shows his face around here, he's in trouble."

Marty laughed. "What are you going to do? Bury him in carrots?"

"I'll bury him in something!" She laughed maniacally, throwing her head back.

"If the kids see you like this, you're going to scar them for life."

"You're right. No need to scare the children. David will get what's coming to him eventually." Lucy put the head on and hopped out onto the patio.

Marty laughed to himself. Life had taken such a strange turn.

He was about to follow her outside when Gigi caught him.

She held up a finger. "I think I have a package for you. Hang on."

She returned a moment later with a small box. Marty thanked her and saw it was postmarked nearly three weeks prior. Apparently, she'd forgotten it for quite some time.

It wasn't a big deal, just some mail that his friend had sent up from his old apartment. There were a few weeks where he hadn't gotten his mail forwarded, and he was only now catching up. He opened the box, sifting through letters from his mom, his old university, and one that he didn't recognize.

There was no return address on the envelope, and it was addressed simply to "Marty." He opened it and began reading the letter inside.

Dear Marty,

I caught you on the FBI's most wanted list last month. You look so much like someone I used to know. I'm here for you if you need me. Take care and stay out of trouble.

Yours,

B

Marty didn't know anyone who went by the initial B.

Claire caught his eye and walked over.

"Are you coming outside?" she asked cheerfully.

"Yeah. I just need to put this in my car."

Claire leaned forward to see what was in his hands, but Marty folded the letter and put everything back in the box.

"What's that?" she asked.

"Nothing, just some old mail." He smiled. "I'll be out in a minute."

She nodded and went outside.

Marty felt bad hiding the letter from her, but he didn't want to freak her out. Ever since he'd been on the FBI's most wanted list, he'd developed a weird sort of fan club.

There weren't many people in this club, but they were passionate. They sent letters to any address they could find for him – his old college, SureFired's office, even the library near his apartment.

It was bizarre. The letters had everything from offers to hide him to offers to marry him. He'd become a minor celebrity, like prisoners sometimes were. One woman declared she was a spy and that she'd happily smuggle him out of the country.

Marty had no time for these shenanigans. Luckily, none of them had found his address on Orcas Island yet. He intended to keep it that way.

He walked out to his car and read the letter again. It made him feel more queasy than the others. He wasn't sure why. Perhaps because this person didn't ask for anything? They just wanted to say hello.

Of course, the letter B made him think of Becca. But that was impossible. It was just another looney letter. He'd add it to the pile and move on with his life.

Marty threw the letters into the passenger seat of his car and locked the door. He wasn't going to miss Lucy hopping around the grounds for anything.

The Next Chapter

Introduction to *Sunset Secrets*

Living in paradise isn't always what it's cracked up to be...

Marty Coursin is finally living the good life. Free of the erroneous FBI charges against him, now he's able to spend his days in comfort on Orcas Island. Sure, there's a bit of a mystery surrounding who's been sending him strange, anonymous messages. But who cares about that when everything is going his way, including the arrival of a beautiful, fascinating new resident?

Emma Dickinson is ready for a fresh start. With her health problems under control and her divorce finalized, island life is exactly what she needs. She won't ever fall in love again, though. Not even with her charming new friend, Marty. No matter how perfect he seems, risking her heart again is not in her best interest. Or so she keeps telling herself...

Will Marty's secretive nature, colorful past, and best intentions only serve to keep Emma at arm's length? Or will she learn to trust – and love – him enough to take a shot at happily ever after?

Sunset Secrets, book two in the Orcas Island series, is a sweet, romantic, contemporary women's fiction read full of joy and second chances. Enjoy the sites of the San Juan Islands through the eyes of your favorite islanders – Marty, Lucy, and Claire. Get your copy today!

Would you like to join my reader group?

Sign up for my reader newsletter and get a free copy of my novella Christmas at Saltwater Cove. You can sign up by visiting: https://bit.ly/XmasSWC

About the Author

Amelia Addler writes always sweet, always swoon-worthy romance stories and believes that everyone deserves their own happily ever after.

Her soulmate is a man who once spent five weeks driving her to work at 4AM after her car broke down (and he didn't complain, not even once). She is lucky enough to be married to that man and they live in Pittsburgh with their little yellow mutt. Visit her website at AmeliaAddler.com or drop her an email at amelia@AmeliaAddler.com.

Also by Amelia...

The Orcas Island Series

Sunset Cove

Sunset Secrets

Sunset Tides

The Westcott Bay Series

Saltwater Cove

Saltwater Studios

Saltwater Secrets

Saltwater Crossing

Saltwater Falls

Saltwater Memories

Saltwater Promises

Christmas at Saltwater Cove

Standalone Novels

The Summer Request

Made in the USA
Monee, IL
09 June 2024

59601291R00152